# CAUTION
### ON ICE

# CAUTION ON ICE

## BOYS OF WINTER #4

# S.R. GREY

Caution on Ice (Boys of Winter #4)
Copyright © 2018 by S.R. Grey

ISBN-13: 978-0-9979749-7-3 (print edition)
ISBN-10: 0-9979749-7-4 (print edition)

Editing: Hot Tree Editing
Proofreading: Deaton Author Services
Cover Photographer: CJC Photography
Model: Burton Hughes
Cover Design: Najla Qamber
Interior Design and Formatting: by:
www.emtippettsbookdesigns.com

# OTHER BOOKS BY
# S.R. GREY

**Boys of Winter series**
*Destiny on Ice*
*Resistance on Ice*
*Complications on Ice*
*Caution on Ice*

**Judge Me Not series**
*I Stand Before You*
*Never Doubt Me*
*Just Let Me Love You*
*The After of Us*

**Inevitability duology**
*Inevitable Detour*
*Inevitable Circumstances*

**Promises series**
*Tomorrow's Lies*
*Today's Promises*

**A Harbour Falls Mystery trilogy**
*Harbour Falls*
*Willow Point*
*Wickingham Way*

**Laid Bare novella series**
*Exposed: Laid Bare 1*
*Unveiled: Laid Bare 2*
*Spellbound: Laid Bare 3*
*Sacrifice: Laid Bare 4*

# GHOSTS FROM THE PAST

## DYLAN

I hail a taxi cruising down the snow-covered road, and as I do, the bitter wind cuts through the thin wool of the long black coat I'm wearing.

*Shit, I should've packed something heavier, a jacket with down maybe.*

I sigh as I remind myself, "Yeah, you should've done a lot of things differently."

Shivering from the cold, or maybe it's from memories creeping in, I wonder how I could've forgotten how cold Buffalo is in late December.

"You, of all people, should have known better."

There are those words again—*should have.*

"Fuck," I bite out. "Why is the goddamn taxi taking so long to get over here?"

Shielding my eyes from the snow blowing around, I squint to find it's stopped at a red light.

*Ah, okay.*

This delay gives me more time to think. But hell, I'd rather not. I'm trying to forget this city was once my home.

It's too late as ragged bits of the past come at me like a freight train. Because of where I'm headed today, a place I'd rather not visit, but I must because it's where the past and the present collide. And who knows? Maybe I'll find some peace.

*Yeah, right.*

I may be in Buffalo for hockey, but my past is here for good, beckoning me, calling me, haunting me.

See, I lived in Buffalo a long time ago, back when I was a boy and not serious at all about the sport I now play professionally. It's funny to think that hockey ultimately saved my ass. If I'd never picked up that first stick, who knows where I'd be today?

Nowhere good, that's for sure.

I wouldn't be what I am—a twenty-seven-year-old Stanley Cup champion, standing on a corner, hailing a cab in a two-thousand-dollar coat.

"A two-thousand-dollar coat that's shit in the cold," I murmur as I shiver some more.

Too bad it's not the freezing cold that's cutting me to the bone. It's not; it's the demons from my past. Those bastards are colder than ice, and unlike this transitory cold, will never go away.

*You should've done more to save her,* one of those demons from the past reminds me now.

"But I was just a kid," I protest to this one, named Guilt.

*That's no excuse,* Guilt hisses in my head.

Thank God the taxi is pulling up. Because I'm really losing it here.

Ice crunches beneath the spinning tires as the cab slides to a slippery stop.

"Hop on in," a young, friendly male driver says when I open the back door.

I jump in and before he can utter another word, which is what it looks like he's gearing up to do, I snap, "Can we just get going already?"

The scruffy kid, who can't be more than nineteen, peers back at me in the rearview mirror.

"Someone chasing you, man?" he wants to know.

"You could say that," I mutter.

"Hey, I don't want any trouble," he says as he twists around to face me, looking worried as hell. "Maybe you should get out and wait for another ride."

"Wait a second, kid. You've been the only cab to drive by in the past twenty minutes. I was freezing my balls off out there."

"There's a hotel down the road," he offers, "and cabs are always lined up outside."

"Yeah, I know." I sigh. "That's where I'm staying."

Before he can ask what I'm doing a mile up the road, and why I didn't just grab a ride at the hotel, plus before he doesn't really kick me out, I try to explain.

"Look, I needed a walk to clear my head. I have a lot on my mind. That's why I'm so desperate to get moving.'"

"Ahh, I see. The walk didn't work, did it? For clearing your head, that is."

"No, it didn't," I say.

"Sorry, man." Totally chill now that he knows I'm not running from the law or something, the driver places the cab in gear. "So where do you want to go?"

"Uh, I need to go to United Cemetery."

Frowning back at me from the mirror, he says, "You know they don't plow much up there this time of year, right?"

"I know, but it's really important I go."

"Okay," he sighs. "I'll give it a shot."

"Thanks."

The kid's pretty quiet as we start out, leaving me with nothing to focus on but *why* I'm going to a snowy cemetery in the dead of winter.

*Fuck, not again.*

I look around to latch onto something—*anything*—to talk about. And wouldn't you know it, hockey comes to the rescue once again when the driver slips on a knit cap that's blue and has a Buffalo Sabres logo.

Quickly, I say, "The Sabres are looking really good this season, yeah?"

Since they're the reason why I'm in town with the Las Vegas Wolves, the team I play for, I know all about them. This is so perfect.

With a big grin, the kid replies, "Yeah, they're playing balls to the wall, man. There's a game tonight and I think it's a lock. I mean, sure, the Wolves are good and all, but they've been struggling lately."

"They sure have," I murmur.

This is all too true. Our team's been in a real slump. We're even dropping in the standings like a goddamn rock.

Ever since one of our best players, forward Nolan Solvenson, got hurt, we can't seem to get it together.

But we better turn it around soon, and fast. Otherwise, we can kiss a second Stanley Cup goodbye.

"You plan on watching the game?" the kid wants to know.

"Uh, you could say that since I'll be there."

"No fucking way! That's super cool, dude."

He glances back at me but clearly doesn't recognize me from the Wolves roster. He thinks I'm just a fan.

If only he know. Maybe I'll tell him before it's all said and done.

Focusing back on the road, he laments, "I haven't been to a game in, like, forever. Seats are just too expensive."

Hell, I can't leave a true hockey fan hanging, even if he will be rooting for the competition.

It's time to come clean. "I could get you a ticket if you want," I murmur.

"Dude…" He laughs. "You must really have some major connections. Do you know a player or something?"

"Funny you should ask," I reply, chuckling.

I share with him then that *I* am a player, and he exclaims, "No fucking way!"

We come to a red light and he turns around to study me, no doubt trying to figure out who I am.

"You must be with the Wolves," he says at last. "I'd recognize you if you were a Sabre."

"I am with the Wolves," I confirm.

"What's your name?"

"Dylan Culderway."

"That's right! Defenseman, top line, I know who you are now."

"You got it."

The light turns green, and he turns back around, muttering as he does, "A professional hockey player in *my* cab"—he shakes his head— "amazing, man."

After a minute, I reiterate about the tickets and he's, of course, all in.

I go on to make the necessary calls while he drives, our destination not far now.

I feel good that I made someone's day, but that feeling doesn't last long as we travel through the open gates of the graveyard.

Somber now, I ask, "Do you mind waiting for me? I shouldn't be all that long."

"Sure." The kid gestures to a clump of birch trees a few yards away. "I'll pull up over there, give you some privacy."

I look ahead at the trees and I'm shivering again. They're white as bone and skeletal without leaves.

*How very appropriate,* I muse.

Before I close the door, I remind the kid, "I'll be back in a few."

He nods and drives away.

Alone again in the cold, and with the ghosts of the past coming back to life, I take a deep breath.

*Fuck, it's freezing.*

I turn away from the wind to start over to where my mother is buried.

My mother who died too young…

My mother who died in front of me…

My mother who died at the hands of my rotten stepfather…

I couldn't stop any of it from happening, and that's what tortures me day in and day out.

If only I could make some sort of amends maybe I'd heal for good. That's what this trip to a bone-chilling graveyard is all about.

Too bad I know it won't help in the end. It never does.

Only thing going to save me now is saving someone else...to succeed where I failed.

I wonder who she'll be.

# 2

# STARTING OVER

## CHLOE

On a day near the end of December, all that's left of my old life is in the rearview mirror.

I mean that quite literally, seeing as my brother, Graham, just moved me up from Phoenix.

A couple of days ago I was there.

And now I'm here in Las Vegas.

I chose this city because my brother lives here. Not to mention, he's the one who talked me into this move. I was hesitant at first, but that all changed on Christmas Eve. Good thing Graham had already found me a place to live. He'd even paid the first two months' rent.

He's a good brother like that. That's why I hope that someday he finds someone who truly appreciates him. He's a prince, and he deserves a worthy princess.

But fairy tales will have to wait for now, and for the both of us.

All these thoughts of princes and princesses have me asking Graham, "Will I ever be happy again?"

He glances up from the laptop he's been pecking away on. "Where's this coming from, Chloe?"

We're both seated on the floor in the living room of the apartment he secured for me. It's not really an apartment, per se; it's one half of an adobe-style duplex. I love it because there are no close neighbors. The tenants in the half connected to mine moved out right before I arrived, and the other units are a ways away from mine.

"I don't know," I say, getting back to his question. "I just hope I made the right decision."

Graham shoots me an are-you-kidding-me look, and I feel compelled to clarify.

"Wait. I know I made the right decision in leaving. There's no question about that. I'm just wondering if I should've stayed in Phoenix."

My brother and I were born and raised there, so, in a way, it'll always be home. He lived there for a long time too, back when he played professional football.

Smiling, he assures me, "Las Vegas will feel like home soon enough."

"Yeah, well, I hope you're right."

Focusing back on whatever he's doing on the laptop, he murmurs, "You need some furniture, Chlo. I think that'll help transition you."

*Aha, that's what he's up to!*

"Hmm, what exactly are you working on over there?"

We've been hanging out on the hardwood floor for over an hour. I've been reading—well, trying to—a romance novel on my Kindle. I think that's why I'm stuck on fairy tales.

Graham turns the laptop so I can see the screen.

"I knew it!" I exclaim.

He's up to exactly what I suspected—ordering me furniture.

I left Phoenix in a hurry, so I am rather light on worldly possessions. Still, I insist, "You don't have to buy me anything. I applied for a job at that coffee shop down the street. So I'll have income rolling in soon enough."

"When did you have time to do that?" he asks. "You just got here two days ago."

I shrug. "What can I say? I move fast. I walked down yesterday and filled out an application."

"Good for you, Chloe. Good for you."

I know he's proud I'm moving on. Graham is all about forward progress, and not just on the football field.

I continue, "They'll probably hire me since I'm twenty-six, not a teenager. I overheard the manager talking to an employee, and she was going on and on about how hard it is to find reliable help these days."

"It sounds like you're in," he says with a nod.

"So, see." I wave my hand around the empty room. "I'll have this place furnished in no time."

"Chloe…" He gives me a look. "Just let me do this for you."

I give in because it makes sense, seeing as it would take a while to save enough to buy as much as I need. He knows this, and so do I.

"Buy away," I say at last.

I confer with him on some things, but let him choose other stuff on his own. Truth is that I trust his judgment. He's four years older than me, and it's always been this way.

Graham is thirty but looks much younger, probably because he rocks surfer-dude good looks—messy blond hair, massive muscles, piercing blue eyes.

It's then that I look up and notice those piercing blue eyes are fixed on me.

"What?" I say.

"I was just asking you a question."

"What question?"

"What size TV would you like?"

"Oh… Wait. Skip the TV. You've done enough for me already."

He has. So far, he's ordered a sofa, two plushy chairs, a coffee table, a dinette set, and a bed.

But Graham insists, "You're getting a TV, Chloe."

He returns to the browser, scrolling away and making me mutter, "Oh, Lord, you're impossible."

"Hmm," he muses, ignoring my commentary, "I think the 75" will look good on your wall."

"And just why do you think I need such a huge TV?" I question.

"To watch porn, of course."

I throw a pillow at him, one of the few things I grabbed from my Phoenix house. And then I politely inform him, "I am not discussing the pros and cons of big-screen porn with you, Graham."

"Trust me, Chloe, there are only pros."

"I am not watching porn on this television!" I yell.

He laughs. "Yeah, right."

I wave the white flag on this battle, because truth is, I might. I also let him go ahead and order the latest model ultra-high-def flat-screen. If I'm going to be watching cocks, they may as well be huge.

After Graham hits the Buy button, he informs me, "On a more serious note, Chlo, you'll definitely want to watch the playoffs on this thing."

He means football. Having played in the pros, he's passionate about the game. He was really good too, a star quarterback for the Cardinals till he blew out his knee. That was bad, really bad, but what was worse was when he ended up addicted to pain meds.

Graham is clean now, though, and has been for three years.

God, I'm so damn proud of him. But proud or not, I need to set him straight on one thing— "If I'm going to be watching any sport on TV, it'll be hockey."

"Ah, yes," he says. "I forgot you're a wannabe puck bunny."

I'd throw another pillow at him, but I'm fresh out.

"You're such an ass," I snort. "You're lucky I love you so much."

"I am your favorite brother, yeah?"

"You're my only brother, goofball."

"And you're my only sister," he says. "But you're still my favorite."

"Aw, that's sweet."

A moment passes with Graham making more purchases.

That prompts me to state, "Hey, I'm totally paying you back for everything you're buying."

"Yeah, yeah, whatever," he mutters distractedly.

Graham will never take a dime from me. He's pretty well-off since he invested his football earnings wisely.

Me? My finances are in shambles. My asshole ex-husband, Sten, made sure of that. That's the reason I called the prick on Christmas Eve and asked him to come over. I wanted to know where our shared savings had gone, all ten thousand of it.

Asking him over was a major mistake, though. When I showed him the statement, the one that proved he'd withdrawn all the money, he laughed in my face.

"What are you going to do about it, you lousy bitch? You try to come after me and I'll make your life a living hell."

He's always threatening me, putting me down, calling me names.

That's why I'd finally had enough. Not only we're we divorced, but that night, I took the statement and threw it in his fucking face.

"Fuck you!" I screamed. "Just fuck you."

I was on a roll, naming off every shitty thing he'd ever done to me, and how I was so happy I'd never have to deal with him ever again.

"Just keep the money!" I yelled. "Having you out of my life is worth every cent."

Too bad I missed his fist coming at me then.

My eye felt like it was exploding, and I saw nothing but white.

When I returned to my senses, I realized Sten had taken off. My phone was on a stand by the door and I grabbed it, all set to call the police and have his ass arrested—finally.

But then I hesitated.

I knew if I pressed charges I'd have to return to Phoenix to testify against him. And by that point, I just wanted out of there. I wanted Sten gone from my life forever.

So I called Graham instead.

"I know it's Christmas Eve," I said, sniffling into the phone. "But can you come to Phoenix tonight and get me out of this goddamn town?"

He knew I was trying hard to hold back the tears, and without asking for any explanation, he said, "Hold tight. I'll be there by midnight."

My brother was perceptive then, and he is now as well.

Peering over at me thoughtfully, he says, "Hey, what's up?"

Feeling suddenly self-conscience, I tug away the tie holding my hair up in a high ponytail and wavy blonde locks fall to frame my face.

But why am I hiding?

Graham has already seen my black eye. He saw it in full purple bloom the night Sten gave it to me.

When he presses again, I confess what's weighing on me. "I feel so stupid about how I ended up. I always swore I'd never be one of *those* girls. Yet here I am, alone and a runaway from a bad life. I'm a damn cliché, Graham."

I start sobbing, and my brother scoots his big body over and drapes a comforting arm around my shoulders.

"Chloe, you're not a cliché. And you're not alone. I'm here for you."

I lean into him. "I know. And thank you."

"Don't be so hard on yourself, okay? Bad relationships happen to the best of us. Sometimes you just end up in too deep before you finally see your way out of it."

I laugh bitterly. "I was so stupid when it came to Sten."

"Hey, at least you were married to him only for a short while. That phony prick could've fooled anyone. He's a charmer when he wants to be and a master manipulator all the time."

"I just really thought he loved me," I sigh. "I never dreamed it'd come to this."

Sten wined and dined me early on, sweeping me off my feet with flowers and presents. He even bought me the car I drive today, a white Ford Fusion. Sadly, there was nothing but emptiness behind all his hollow gestures. I saw that the first time he was mean to me.

"I should've left the first time he ever put me down, Graham."

My brother doesn't disagree, though he tries to put a positive spin on things. "You're just a really sweet person, Chloe. You see the best in everyone, and you're very forgiving."

"Too forgiving," I snort as I sit up straight. Pointing to the ugly bruising all around my eye, I add, "To my own detriment, clearly."

Through clenched teeth, Graham says, "I swear I should've found that prick and kicked his ass before we left Phoenix."

My brother is a better judge of character than me. He never liked Sten. He told me before I eloped, after a whirlwind courtship, that I should hold off.

I realized he'd been right when Sten first started with the insults…

"You're not that smart, now are you, Chloe?" soon escalated to, "You're a fucking worthless bitch, whore."

His wicked words were a whirlwind, like our courtship, and soon I was numb to the jabs. Sten had worn me down. I believed what he drilled in my head—that his berating was somehow my fault. If I could just do better, be prettier, lose weight, I would be a better wife, and then I'd have the marriage I longed for.

I consoled myself with one thing at the time—*at least he doesn't hit me.*

He didn't, either…till he did.

That was finally the end for me.

I'd grown a backbone, and I vowed that weak woman would never be me again. I filed for divorce that day.

Christmas Eve was my only mistake. I never should've asked Sten to come over, not when I was alone.

I only wish now that I could have a little payback, even if it were just symbolically.

With that in mind, I say to Graham, "You know what? I'm not only mad, I'm like really freaking furious."

"You should be, Chloe. You have every right to be pissed as hell."

Riled up, I growl, "Damn it, I know it's not right, but I'd love to punch Sten in his stupid face. Just once, for all the grief he's given me."

"You clearly need to let off some steam or find an outlet of some sort."

"I should probably just focus on moving forward first."

"That's a process too," Graham reminds me. And then he says, "Oh, yeah, I almost forgot."

Leaning forward, he reaches into his jeans pocket and fishes out what looks to be a small pamphlet. "I have something for you," he says.

Taking the pamphlet from his outreached hand, I ask, "What is it?"

"It's nothing big, but it might help you move on."

I flip through the pages of what appears to be a self-help pamphlet. I'm not surprised Graham picked this up for me. Having gone through rehab, he's all about the twelve steps. Or ten, as this one happens to be.

"I grabbed it at a meeting last week," he explains. "There were bunches lying on a table, booklets on all sorts of subjects. But that one made me think of you."

"Thank you," I reply, feeling truly appreciative.

My brother stays sober by attending NA meetings regularly. His commitment to helping others keeps him on the straight and narrow. That's why he's a sponsor too.

His kindness clearly extends to me. This is Graham helping me. As if he hasn't done enough.

"'X Your Ex,'" I murmur, reading the title aloud. "This certainly is the perfect self-help guide for me."

"I know, right? That's what I thought too."

"Well, hell, I think I'll start it today," I announce.

Graham looks pleased as he leans in. "So what's step one? I didn't check them out in advance."

"Hmm, let's see…" I flip to the beginning of the booklet. "Step one is, uh… Oh my God, Graham, you're going to love this one. It's 'Stop

Taking Shit.'"

We look at each other and burst out laughing.

This is so perfect.

Since I'm already toughening up mentally, I declare, "I know what I'm going to do to complete this one."

"Oh, yeah, what's that?"

"I'm going to work on getting stronger. That way I can stop taking shit like a mofo next time someone comes at me."

"I love it," Graham says. "A few self-defense lessons would do you a world of good."

Thinking of how it would have surprised the shit out of Sten had I fought back, I agree and ask Graham, "Can you teach me?"

"You bet. We can even practice at my gym."

Graham just happens to own a small, nondescript workout facility. It's like a gritty gym straight out of *Rocky*.

"Hey, I'm ready to go a few rounds," I say. "When can we start?"

"Anytime you want."

I feel good. Graham's gym is the perfect place to learn how to defend myself. The clientele are mostly friends and associates of his. My brother is super selective on whom he lets in, so I'll surely feel at ease even when he's not around.

Standing victoriously—I like this new me—I declare, "Okay, step one in the X Your Ex program is officially underway. You have heavy bags there, right?"

"Several."

"Good because I plan to beat the hell out of each and every one. And the whole time I'm going to imagine Sten's stupid face."

Grinning up at me, Graham says, "I'll do you one better, little sis."

I'm curious as to what he has in mind, so I raise a brow and ask,

"Yeah, how so?"

"I'm going to print out some head shots of that douchebag and paste them to all the bags."

"I love it, Graham. That's the best idea I've heard all day. Sten is going down!"

I can't wait. Even if this is only happening in the gym, I know punching the hell out of that bastard is going to feel amazing.

# UNDER PRESSURE

## DYLAN

After spending the afternoon at the cemetery, freezing my balls off amid a flood of memories that kept bubbling up to the surface, I'm in no mood for bullshit when the game against the Buffalo Sabres gets underway.

But bullshit is all I get.

Like when we're on the power play. I'm positioned at point because so many of the shots I take from the blue line go in the net.

Not tonight, though. Nope, tonight fucking fate has conspired against me. Even when our captain, Brent Oliver, flips the puck right onto my goddamn stick, I fan on the ensuing shot.

*What the hell?*

I am a wreck this evening.

A Sabres' forward intercepts the next puck I handle, and though I pursue him with a vengeance, he out-skates me.

*Shit.*

The fucker burns me and scores a shorthanded goal.

*Fuck, it's going from bad to worse.*

The Buffalo crowd goes nuts. Their cheers echo in my ears like a bad soundtrack to my poor play as I skate back over to the bench.

Tossing my stick behind everyone, I grind out, "Motherfucking shit. That puck-stealing pussy—"

"Culderway, that's enough," Coach Townsend interjects, shooting me a disappointed look since I'm never like this. "Focus on the next shift," he goes on. "Leave that one behind."

He's right, but I can't help but mutter a dejected, "Whatever."

Benny Perry, a first-line forward—and one of my best friends on the team, along with Nolan Solvenson—is seated on the bench next to me.

Leaning in, he hisses, "Coach T's already in a miserable mood, Dylan. We're down three to one. Now's not the time to get on his bad side."

Benny should know what it's like to be on Coach Townsend's bad side—he's fucking his daughter. I say as much, and he peers over at me like "What the fuck?"

"Dude," he snarls, "Coach and I worked that shit out. And for the record, what Eliza and I have is *way* more than fucking. You know that."

I do, it's true.

Shit, there's no reason for me to be taking out my frustrations on my friend.

"Sorry," I murmur. "I shouldn't have said that."

"What's gotten into you, anyway?" Benny questions. "You're never like this."

I shrug. "I don't know."

But I do know. That visit to my mom's final resting place has dredged up how she ended up there in the first place. And now all I can think about is *who* put her there—my fucking stepfather. I keep seeing *his* face on every opponent.

That's why, when I'm back on the ice, it's no real surprise I get into a fight.

*This isn't me*, I tell myself. And it's not. I'm not a fucking goon. I'm a premiere defenseman, an elite player who skates fast and scores loads of goals. Hell, I'm currently ranked the number one defenseman in the league, despite our decline in the standings. That's how good I am. For Christ's sake, I won the Norris trophy last year!

None of that sets me right, though. I continue to taunt players for no good reason, one in particular. I'm shocked I don't draw a penalty when I hook that particular guy. Getting away with that encourages me to stay on his ass and trash-talk him.

Why am I all up in this dude's grill?

One reason and one reason only—he's kind of small and has a mustache like *he* did.

Yeah, resembling my asshole stepfather is reason enough for me.

When the player gets fed up with my shit, he takes a swing.

Finally!

This is what I want, so I throw off my gloves and start pummeling him.

I would've done this if I could have "back then." If only I'd been a little bit older, I could've saved my mom. Too bad I was just a scrawny little kid.

*I'm no scrawny kid now, though,* I remind myself as I clock the dude with a mean right hook.

A linesman skates over to break up the fight, but I'm having none of that.

"Just let us go!" I yell at him.

"Fucking fine," the official barks back. He backs off and adds, "Have at it, boys."

We do. We have at it hard.

'Stashe Guy gets in a couple of decent hits, but I'm the one who draws first blood when I crack open his nose.

"Shit, Culderway," the dude says, stunned.

Wow, I give him props. He's handling it well for a guy gushing blood.

The linesman breaks us apart then, even though we've pretty much stopped fighting anyway. Penalties are then assessed, and since it's late in the game, I just skate off the ice and head down the runway to the locker room.

The rest of the team files in a short while later, but I ignore them. I shower and dress without speaking to anyone. It's like they all know my head's not in a good place so they let me be.

Not Coach Townsend, though. He wants to see me out in the hallway.

Pulling me aside when I step out of the locker room, he grinds out, "What the hell's going on with you, Dylan?"

Shrugging, I reply, "Nothing, really."

He knows that's not true.

"This isn't like you, Culderway. Not one little bit. Something's not right."

I sigh and finally admit, "I have some personal stuff going on, Coach."

"No shit," he scoffs. "Is it anything you'd like to talk about?"

"Nope."

He pats me on the shoulder. "Okay, I'm not going to press. But…" He pulls out a business card from his suit pocket and hands it to me. "I think you should check this place out. It may help relieve some of your stress."

*Huh?*

I look down at the card. It's pretty plain, with just the name of some workout place—*Graham Tettersaw's Private Gym*—printed on it, along with a phone number and an address.

The pieces come together then.

"Wait, I know that name. Graham's that football player who blew out his knee a couple of years ago, right? Played for the Arizona Cardinals, I believe."

"That's right," Coach confirms. "He's a good friend of Benny's and owns a gym where a lot of athletes like to go to work out."

"You think that's what I need?" I laugh. "You really think me working out more will solve my problems?"

"It can't hurt, Culderway. All that excess aggression I saw on the ice tonight makes me think this particular gym could be the perfect place for you. You can work out whatever it is that's been bothering you lately in a private environment away from the team."

Ah, I see what he's doing—Coach doesn't want my negative attitude affecting the team.

But I'm not sure this is the right move, so I try to hand the card back to him.

"Look, Coach, I appreciate this, I do. But really, I'm good."

Pushing the card back to me, he says, "Dylan, I've been around a long time, and what I saw out there looked like rage brewing just beneath the surface. It's trying to take hold, son. I've seen this before with other guys, and I'm telling you, it's best to address these issues before they become a huge problem."

"I know," I quietly concede.

Coach knows *why* I have rage brewing beneath the surface. I may bury the past, but everyone knows what happened. You can't be famous and keep shit like that a secret. Not to mention I'm not exactly quiet about it. I donate money and a shit-ton of my time to organizations that advocate for victims of domestic abuse.

It's the least I can do for failing my mom.

I may seem like a man who's come out ahead of a bad situation, but the truth is I still struggle. Visiting the cemetery made things worse, not better, just as I knew it somehow would.

Coach is right—I need to get a handle on this. I have to get back to being me. You can't let the ghosts of the past hold you back. Isn't that what I'm always telling everyone?

So, at last, as I pocket the card, I say, "You're right, Coach T. I need to face this crap head on before it becomes unmanageable."

His brows go up. "So you'll call the gym?"

"Yes, I will."

Clapping me on the back, he says, "You're a good man, Dylan."

Let's just hope he's right.

# K-Y JELLY AND ONE NECESSARY LIE

## CHLOE

**W**hack. Whack. Whack.

"A little lower, Chloe," Graham instructs. "That's good, but you're getting in nothing but shots to the head. You need to go for the throat. Like this…"

He shows me exactly where to hit, and I follow suit.

"That's a vulnerable spot on everyone," he goes on to say, just as I dead-center throat-punch an imaginary Sten.

Graham, as promised, taped pics of the dickhead to several bags. I've punched and pounded all of them off, except this one. It remains… but not for long.

Whack. Whack. Whack.

And there it goes, fluttering to the floor. "Yes!"

I step back away from the bag, feeling pretty damn good about myself.

And then I feel even better as I stomp all over Sten.

*Ha!* "Not so fast, bud. You're not getting away that easily," I mutter as I grind a toe into his nose.

Back to imagining *he's* the bag, I knee imaginary-Sten at groin level.

Graham lets out a low whistle as he covers his own junk.

"Whoa, I wouldn't want to run into you in a dark alley, Chlo. You're a natural at this."

"I'll take that as a compliment, coming from you, big bro." I lean against the bag and catch my breath. "Damn, I'm feeling empowered already," I remark.

"Stop taking shit, right?"

"You got it."

Lifting weights, punching the crap out of things, and learning to fight has been good for me. It's also left me with a feeling I haven't experienced in quite some time—interest in meeting someone new.

Since Graham is so picky about who can come and work out in his gym, I know anyone I meet here will most likely be a good dude.

*So why not look around?*

I scan around and whoa!

Wouldn't you know it; there is someone who catches my eye—a tall, good-looking muscular guy lifting weights across the room.

"Oh, my," I murmur.

With cheekbones you could cut ice on, a strong jaw, and lush dark hair, he is absolutely gorgeous.

But it's his made-for-sin body that makes me ask Graham, "Who the heck is that?"

"Chloe…" He laughs as I discreetly—or so I hope—jerk my chin hot guy's way. "That's Dylan Culderway. And it's funny you should notice him."

"Hmm, why's that?"

"Let's just say that Dylan Culderway is definitely your kind of guy."

"Clearly," I reply. "Just look at the way his muscles bulge enticingly under that T-shirt."

Graham rolls his eyes. "I didn't mean *that*, pervy girl. I meant he's your kind of guy because he plays hockey."

"What?" I grab his arm. "Please tell me you're not joking. This isn't payback for that time I put K-Y in your hair gel, is it?"

"Chloe, that was over twelve years ago."

"Still, you were really mad, Graham."

"Of course I was angry! I was about to go out on a date with that crap in my hair. And you were going to let me. You only fessed up when my head got real hot."

I cringe. "Yes, I was worried your hair might fall out. Or that you'd suffer irreparable scalp damage."

"Yeah, that was bizarre. I still can't figure out why K-Y jelly did that."

"Uh, maybe because it was the warming kind," I sheepishly reply.

"Ugh." Graham makes a face. "Why'd you even have shit like that at *fourteen*?"

"It wasn't mine," I protest. "It was Mom's."

"Oh, Christ, that's even worse."

I wave my hand around. "Enough! Let's get back to Dylan. Does he play hockey or not?"

Graham raises a brow. "Shouldn't you know the answer to that, puck bunny?"

"I am not a puck bunny!" I yell, which makes the man in question glance over.

*Great, busted.*

I turn so my back's to Dylan and hiss to Graham, "For your information, smartass, I've only had time to watch one Wolves game. I don't know their whole roster yet."

"Okay, okay. Don't beat me up. In fact, you can just ask him yourself. He's coming over."

"WHAT?"

I roll my head to the right to discover Dylan is indeed heading this way.

*Eek!* All my head-rolling and chin jerking, not to mention the puck bunny comment, have probably come off as mating signals, because here…he…comes.

*No, I'm all sweaty and gross. This is not the time to meet a hot hockey player.*

I grab Graham's arm and plead, "Save me?"

"Ha," he replies, vengeful and smug. "Not a chance. You're on your own, Miss K-Y."

He starts walking away and I call out, "I thought you weren't still mad about that? You said yourself it was over twelve years ago."

Too late, Graham's retreated to the neutral zone—the men's locker room.

And the hockey player is closing in.

I turn to face him, flipping my ponytail and flashing my most winning smile.

"Hi," I breathe out, adding in a cute wave for good measure.

But it's all for naught—gorgeous Dylan walks right by me like I'm not even there.

I realize then he was on his way to the locker room the whole time.

He wasn't coming over to meet me, not at all.

I'm mortified. I've just made the biggest fool of myself.

And then it gets worse—he turns back around like it just dawned on him I said something.

"Did you just say hi to me?" he asks from a few feet away.

He's so mesmerizingly handsome that all I can do is murmur, "Uh-huh."

His eyes, a rich complex brown, scan me from head to toe. So I go ahead and do the same to him. Now that he's closer it's clear he has a really cool tattoo that starts at his left bicep and continues up to his muscular shoulder. From there, it disappears around to his back. Though I can't see the whole thing, I can tell it's a dragon.

*Hmm, a symbol of strength*, I think to myself. *A strong friend would be good to have.*

And how very timely, seeing as the next step in the X Your Ex program is "Make a New Friend."

Too bad it's not "Have a Night of Wild Sex with a Hot Dude." I could get on board with that one. But then again, maybe not since that's not really me.

"So friends it is," I mumble under my breath.

"What's that?" he says. "I couldn't hear you."

Suddenly, I realize I *have* seen him before—on the big-ass TV Graham bought me. He *is* a hockey player, and a really good one at that. Graham wasn't messing with me. It's just taken me a few minutes to place the name and put it with the face.

And, oh, what a face…

Back to Graham, I feel bad now. Sighing, I say, "Jeez, maybe I shouldn't have brought up the K-Y."

Uh-oh, I just said that a little too loudly. Dylan heard, for sure. The smirk on his face leaves no doubt.

Oh, great. Now he's going to think I'm a nut, a weirdo, and a pervert, all rolled into one. I'm really batting a thousand here.

"K-Y?" He raises a brow. "Should I even ask?"

Chuckling, I reply, "No, probably not. I was just thinking about my brother."

*Oh, crap!*

Now he's eyeing me like I'm some sort of sicko.

Now I'm a nutty weirdo pervert who associates K-Y jelly with her brother.

Ready to melt into the floor, I say, "Can we just start this whole conversation over?"

"Sure," he says, laughing and sticking out his hand. "Hi, I'm Dylan."

I shake his hand and reply, "Hey, Dylan. I'm Chloe, Chloe Tettersaw."

"Ah, so your Graham's sister. You just moved up from Phoenix, right?"

"Yes and yes," I confirm.

This is going much better, so I step closer to him, closing the few feet gap that was separating us.

But wait, what's wrong?

Why is he staring at my face all funny-like?

And then it hits me—*Shit, my black eye!*

There's still some bruising, which Dylan couldn't see from where he was standing.

"Um," I murmur, "you're probably wondering what happened to me, huh?" *Think fast!* I jerk my thumb to the heavy bag. "That damn thing swung back and hit me in the face. Can you believe it? I swear I'm such a klutz sometimes."

With the way his brow is furrowed, I know he doesn't buy it. In fact, something tells me he *knows* that's not what happened. Graham would never tell him; I think he's just intuitive…and smart.

I meet his gaze, and his eyes are questioning.

But mine are pleading, pleading for him not to ask for the truth.

Thank God, he doesn't.

His gaze softens and fills with empathy, making me wonder what he sees.

*Does he see my pain? Can he see the broken parts of me?*

*Fix me, Dylan. Rescue me.*

But wait, what am I thinking? I just met this guy. Still, crazy as it seems, there's no denying there's some kind of connection between us, a connection that was forged in an instant when he saw my black eye.

"Um…" I look away and the spell is broken—for now. "I should go hit the showers."

"Yeah, okay, sure."

I start to leave, but then I turn around. I'm not scared-Chloe anymore, so I state, "I hope to see you around, Dylan."

"I hope so too, Chloe."

Ah, I got him hooked, I can see it in his eyes, hear it in his tone. I think I've done more than "make a friend."

And you know what? That's perfectly fine with me.

# 5

# A CHANCE

## DYLAN

Chloe Tettersaw is intriguing to me on so many levels. Not only is she quirky and funny and sexy and sweet, but she's the first woman I've felt any sort of connection with in ages.

Shit, this is going to sound corny, but I really think she wants someone to save her.

Fuck, I can be that guy.

But first I'd better run it past Graham. I'd hate to be macking on his sister and piss him off. Those two seem close.

I mean, if they joke around about K-Y jelly, they must be tight, right?

Nonetheless, it sure is wild to think Graham and Chloe are brother and sister. Talk about opposites. They may have the same blue eyes and blonde hair, but that's where the similarities end.

Graham is big and strong, a force to be reckoned with. You feel power rolling off him. Chloe is tiny and vulnerable. And she seems kind of…damaged.

The black eye didn't help dispel that impression.

But don't think for a minute I buy that crap about her being klutzy. That black eye was from a punch. Plus, it wasn't recent. It was healing, not a fresh injury.

Who the fuck hit her, though?

And why hasn't Graham killed the guy?

Maybe he has and that's why Chloe's in Vegas? They could be on the run.

Nah, they're not.

Unfortunately, I'm pretty sure the fucker who blasted her is walking the streets, probably somewhere down in Phoenix.

Suddenly, I feel a rage start to build. I hate motherfuckers who hit women—for obvious reasons.

But I need to calm down. I've gotten the issues that were plaguing me back under control. I need to keep it that way.

Since my workouts at Graham's have worked wonders, I should probably head over there now and get in a few reps with the free weights.

Oh, let's not lie. My real reason for wanting to work out is I'm hoping to run into Chloe.

So I go to the gym. But she's not there.

*Damn.*

Determined more than ever now, I start hitting up Graham's gym *a lot*. I even switch over my workouts at the Wolves's training facility and start doing them at the gym.

Coach doesn't care so long as I stay in prime playing shape, which

I do. My extra work shows on the ice, and soon the team starts to turn things around.

But it's not all me and my improved efforts that catapult us up in the standings. Management makes a key trade and we start winning games again.

I'm happy, but not really. Truth is that there's something missing in my life. I still feel empty and alone, and frankly, I'm sick of it.

*Why haven't I run into Chloe?*

That's it. I decide to take matters into my own hands. Life is like that sometimes. You have to go out and get what you want.

And I want Chloe.

I check with Graham, and he tells me his sister has been going to the gym in the evenings. She got a job at a local coffee shop and works mostly mornings and afternoons.

"Ah, got it," I say.

Since he's looking at me oddly, I go ahead and take the opportunity to make sure he's cool with me pursuing his sister.

"Is it okay if I ask her out?" I say softly.

Graham looks surprised at first, but then kind of pleased.

"Yeah, sure," he says. "I don't mind. Just…"

He trails off, and I prompt, "Just what?"

Scrubbing his hand down his face, he says, "Just take it slowly with her, okay? She's been through a lot."

Carefully, I inquire, "Does this have anything to do with that black eye she was sporting?"

"Man, that's not my story to tell. You need to ask Chloe about that."

"Understood," I reply.

I may not have gotten much info out of Graham, but at least I have his blessing to ask his sister out on a date.

I adjust my gym schedule accordingly, and next time I'm there, so is Chloe.

*Finally!*

She's over at the heavy bags—no surprise there. She's going at it hard too, punching away in a series of flurries.

I then notice what seems to have her extra motivated—there's a man's face taped to the bag.

*Wonder if that's the black eye giver?*

"If so, go to town, girl," I murmur.

I lean against the wall and watch from across the room. She's amazing in her anger. Plus, sexy as hell in the black yoga pants and matching crop top she's wearing.

Chloe's soft and curvy in some places, but tight and toned in others. Nonetheless, it's the swell of her breasts and the shape of her ass that has me at attention. In more ways than one, as there's an all-too-familiar tugging in my groin.

That gets me moving.

Chloe's still wailing away on the bag with the guy's face taped to it when I reach her. Her back is turned so she hasn't seen me approach. Since I don't want to sound like a creepy letch, lest I become the next dude taped to the bag, I leave he be and think about what I should say first.

It's been over a week since we met, and I don't want to blow that cool connection we had.

I could ask her if she'd like some water—she does look sweaty and parched—but in the end, I just go with a simple, "Hey."

Chloe spins around, her hand going to her heart. "Oh, Dylan," she breathes out. "You just startled the crap out of me."

"Shit, I'm sorry."

*That was smooth. Not.*

Smiling, she says, "It's okay. I was a little preoccupied."

"Yeah, I noticed that."

"Hmm…"

Thumbing to the picture taped to the heavy bag, which is crumpled all to hell and torn at one corner, I ask, "Who's the guy? Does he deserve that same punishment in person?"

"You could say that," she replies. "He's my ex-husband."

Ah, now it all makes sense. This douche is why she moved up from Phoenix.

"Recently divorced?" I ask.

"Yes, but really, the relationship was over long before the papers were ever signed."

"I get that," I say. And I do—Chloe was married to a real jerk.

"Ugh, that's enough about him." She blows out a frustrated breath as she rips down the pic, crumples it to a ball, and lobs it into a nearby trash can.

"Nice shot," I remark when it circles the can, then goes in.

"Thanks," she says.

I then say, "Think you're up for taking a little break from kicking ex's asses? We could grab some waters and head outside. It's a beautiful evening, and I noticed coming in that your brother set up some picnic tables out back."

"I think I'd like that, Dylan," she replies.

We grab two bottled waters and head out back, where we choose a table situated under a clump of palm trees. It's nice. The fronds make a comforting rustling noise every time there's a breeze.

I kick off the conversation by asking Chloe how she likes Las Vegas, so far.

"It's fine," she says rather unenthusiastically.

"That doesn't sound convincing," I reply.

"I know." Groaning, she adds, "Can I be honest?"

"Sure."

"The truth is it's been kind of lonely since I got here." She looks over at me from across the table and there's sadness in her gaze. "I don't really know anyone besides Graham."

I try to cheer her up by reminding her, "Hey, you know me now."

"Yes, I do. And I'm definitely happy about that."

Hmmm, she looks open for more. So I take a deep breath and go on to ask what I've wanted to since we first sat down. "Would you want to do something with me sometime?"

I mean go out on a date, but she misunderstands.

"Sure, that'd be fun. It'd be nice to have a friend up here in Vegas."

I can't hide my disappointment.

"So you just want to be…*friends*?"

"Is that okay?"

I think about it and decide that sure, I can be friends with her. She did just get out of a bad relationship. I can't expect her to be up for more than friendship…at least for a while.

"Friends work for me," I reply.

"Okay, good."

Then she starts laughing, and I have to say, "Hey, I didn't know friendship was so funny."

She finally composes herself. "Oh, Dylan, I'm sorry. It's not, not usually. But for a second there, it struck me that we sounded like we're in sixth grade."

She's right, and I say, "It never really changes all that much, does it?"

"No, it doesn't," she agrees. Then she clears her throat and says, "Okay, new friend, you know a bunch of stuff about me. It's time I hear a little more about you."

"Fuck. I'm boring as hell," I scoff.

"Ha, I doubt that. You play professional hockey."

"That's true, I do."

"Well, see, that's not boring at all."

I raise a tentative brow. "Do you like hockey?"

"Are you kidding? I freaking *love* hockey."

*Could this woman be any more perfect?*

"That's good to hear," I say, "seeing as hockey is pretty much my whole life."

"I bet."

"Though it can be grueling sometimes, I wouldn't have it any other way."

Smiling, she says, "I'm sure all the perks make it well worth it."

"What do you mean by perks?" I ask, curious to hear her impressions of the hockey life.

"Well, there must be many," she begins. "Besides all the money and fame, I'm sure you Wolves's players have tons of adoring fans."

"I don't know about tons." I laugh. "But the ones we have are amazing."

"Plus, there's the crazier stuff too," she goes on.

"Like…?"

"Well, I bet you have women throwing themselves at you all the time. And you probably go to some pretty wild parties."

I start laughing, and she says, "Hey, what's so funny about that?"

"It's just that my life is so different than what you're imagining,

Chloe. I mean, sure, some players live that way. But I'm not one of them."

"So, womanizing is not for you?"

"Not at all, I'm a one-woman kind of guy."

"And no wild parties every night?"

"Not since my rookie days."

"Jeez, Dylan," she teases, "what do you do for fun?"

I think it over. "Hmm, good question."

She makes a show of placing her hand over her heart. "Oh my God, this is tragic. But I think I have a solution."

If it involves her, I'm in. Still, I should find out what she has in mind.

I ask her as much, and she replies, "I'm inviting you over to my place for dinner, officially, as of right now. And I'm going to make it a good time. I'll whip us up some killer margaritas and we can get crazy buzzed. Then we'll do something really, *really* fun."

I raise a brow. I can think of a *lot* of really fun things to do with Chloe, buzzed or not.

She must read my mind, as she's quick to clarify, "Platonic fun, Dylan."

"Platonic, drunken fun, okay," I retort, chuckling. "I'm down with that."

What I don't add is that I'm down with that *for now*.

Ultimately, I want Chloe. Not just in my bed, though that's a goal too. But what I really want is to show her what it's like to date someone who's not an asshole.

She deserves flowers and orgasms, not black eyes and disappointment.

# 6

# DIABLO CHICKEN AND A CONFESSION

## CHLOE

There's so much more to Dylan than a great body and a handsome face. He really seems like an amazing guy.

I do a little research and find out it's not just wishful thinking. He really *is* a great guy. There's a ton of stuff on the Wolves's website about his involvement with helping victims of domestic abuse.

*Wow, that makes me like him even more.*

All of the players are involved in some sort of charitable work, but Dylan seems to have committed more time and more money than any of the others. I wonder then if there's more to his advocacy.

"I need to find out," I declare.

All of this research is conducted in my kitchen, where I'm also trying to decide what to make for our big dinner, which is tonight.

Having Dylan over is about more than just getting to know him better, though that's a goal too. I'm also up to step three in the X Your Ex program, and it is "Find a New Recipe and Share it with a Friend."

I have the friend, and we're all set to share, so now I need to find a recipe that'll knock said friend's socks off.

"Here goes nothing," I murmur as I close out my Dylan research and google "best tasting recipes."

Turns out, there are many. But one called *diablo chicken* catches my eye. The pictures look so good, what with all the peppers and such .But it's obviously a spicy entrée, so I should make sure Dylan likes hot stuff before I move forward.

I grab my phone, scroll to his number, and hit Call. He picks up right away, which I take as a good sign. "Hey, Chloe, what's up?"

Even better, my name is clearly in his contacts.

"It's not a bad time, is it?" I ask.

"No, not at all, we just finished up with practice."

"Oh, good. I won't keep you, though. I just had a quick question about dinner tonight."

"I'm looking forward to it," he says. "I promise to be good and hungry."

"Great."

*Uh-oh, the pressure to get this right is on.*

"So how do you feel about spicy foods? Do you love them or hate them?"

"I *love* hot stuff," he replies.

*Hmm, I bet he does. Chloe, get your mind out of the gutter. Didn't you tell him you just want to be friends?*

Yes, I did, so I quickly get back to the main conversation.

"That's good to hear," I say. "The entrée I have in mind is called diablo chicken, so…" I shrug even though he can't see me. "…make of that what you will."

"Sounds like we're in for one hell of a night," he jokes.

He's such a sweetie.

We wrap up, and I head out to buy what I need.

Later, just as Dylan's game is underway, I start prepping the ingredients for *diablo chicken*. There are hot peppers to chop, red onions to dice, and chicken to pound.

"At least something's getting pounded." I giggle as I pick up a meat mallet.

As I whack away at the chicken, I think about how I've never been happier than I am right now that I let Graham buy me the massive TV. I mean, wow, Dylan and his teammates are ultra big and clear, even from where I'm working over at the counter.

Once the chicken is in the oven, I start on the margaritas. I pull out the blender, grab the mix I bought at the store, and locate a bottle of tequila I purchased right after I moved in.

The original plan was to crack the bottle open some lonely evening. It's so much better that I have someone to share it with.

But second thoughts arise when I discover how strong it is.

"110 proof!" I exclaim as I read the label. "We're going to be rocked."

Hmm, but a loosened-up Dylan may not be a bad thing. He just may open up about why he's so committed to all those domestic abuse causes.

"So, margaritas it is," I declare.

A short while later, there's another reason to have drinks—to celebrate, seeing as the Wolves just won the game.

Dylan arrives in a great mood. He looks pretty great too, all dressed in dark pants, shiny shoes, and a crisp white button-down.

I stand in the doorway, staring at him for a good, solid minute before letting him in.

He chuckles as he steps into the living room, but then he gives me a thorough once-over and says appreciatively, "You look beautiful tonight, Chloe. That dress is stunning on you."

"Oh, this old thing…" I feign nonchalance. "I threw it on without even thinking."

Totally not true. I knew a sexy black dress would garner his attention.

The oven timer then goes off, and I hurry to the kitchen.

Dylan, following me, remarks, "It smells great in here."

"I hope you like everything."

"I'm sure I will."

When I'm struggling with the roaster, he grabs a pot holder and says, "Here, let me help you."

Between the two of us, we get dinner on the table in no time. And then, in the small dining area off the kitchen, we eat spicy chicken while sipping on margaritas.

Wow, Dylan wasn't lying. He freaking loves the diablo chicken.

Me, I like the chicken. But I love the margaritas even more. Or rather, I love the way they make me feel—uninhibited.

I ditch the "friends" bull and start flirting. Dylan responds positively, which should make me feel great. But it doesn't. The alcohol makes me melancholy, and I start ruminating over things Sten used to say.

And just like that, my confidence crumbles.

I am not this carefree and flirtatious.

I am not someone who's never been put down, never been hit.

Choked up, I stand suddenly and say, "I should clean up this mess."

Sten always hated when I left dishes on the table. But poor Dylan, he just looks confused.

"Is something wrong?" he asks.

I sit back down and put my face in my hands, trying to pull myself together.

"Nothing's wrong," I say at last. "I just need a minute."

*Don't cry, don't cry. Don't ruin this night.*

I look up and God, Dylan looks really worried. "Chloe, seriously, what's wrong?"

"I'm sorry," I quietly state. "I just can't be *that* girl."

"I don't know what that even means. But for the record, I like the girl you *are* just fine."

"Oh, Dylan…"

Now I really want to cry. No, I think I'd rather scream. Or better yet, maybe Dylan can hold me. No, he should leave me alone.

I'm clearly a mess, and that is exactly what I wanted to avoid. It's what I meant when I said *I can't be that girl.*

"I'm damaged," I murmur. "It's true. It's just the damn truth."

"I don't understand why you're saying that," Dylan replies, sounding miffed.

"It's just, this is my fault." I start shaking my head. "I'm ruining our night."

"You're not."

"Riiight."

Our eyes meet then, and there's such gentleness in his gaze that I must look away. I don't deserve this kind of kindness and understanding. Despite his words to the contrary, I *am* screwing up this night, because *I'm* screwed up, *so* screwed up.

*But Dylan is safety,* a little voice says. *He can protect you.*

*From anything, though? Even the past?*

I need to talk to him and share with him why I'm so upset. It's funny how I was thinking earlier that plying him with alcohol would get *him* to open up. Yet here I am, buzzed and wanting nothing more than to share my life.

Or at least, my secrets. I feel like I have to be honest. Friendship, or whatever our future holds, Dylan deserves the truth before we move forward in any kind of way.

So I start with the black eye, which is healed completely, though maybe not so much when it comes to my soul.

"The heavy bag didn't swing back and hit me," I confess.

Dylan sighs. "I figured as much."

"Someone punched me," I whisper.

His cheek twitches. "Who hit you, Chloe?"

"My ex. It wasn't the first time, either. But it was the last"

"Fuck."

He says nothing more, so I venture a glance up to see why.

Oh, no, Dylan looks like he's ready to kill someone.

I better fix this fast.

# 7

# YOU SPIN ME RIGHT ROUND

## DYLAN

I don't want to scare Chloe, especially not after hearing about what her ex used to do.

I close my eyes and run my hand down my face. I need to hold it together, and I think the best way to do that would be to share with Chloe why what she just told me affects me so much.

I take a deep breath, and then I begin.

"You know I do a lot of charity work for victims of domestic abuse, right? Surely, Graham has told you."

"He hasn't said anything," she replies. "But I saw a lot about your work on the Wolves's website."

"Okay…" I reach across the table and squeeze her hand. "There's a reason why I fight so hard for those victims. And it's why hearing stories like yours gets to me so much. It hits too fucking close to home."

"What do you mean?"

Hell, there's something about Chloe Tettersaw that compels me to open up about things I never really talk about. It must be the connection we have, the one I felt in the beginning, and the one that keeps getting stronger.

Still, it doesn't make this any easier.

"I have to stand," I announce, releasing her hand. "I just can't think straight sitting down."

"I understand," she says.

She's so infinitely patient, never once pressing. Not even when I start pacing like a caged lion.

Finally, I head over to the fireplace in the living room and rest my arm on the mantel.

Turning to her, I say, "There's no way for me to sugarcoat this."

"Okay, so don't."

I take a deep breath and release it slowly.

And then I say, "I'm the way I am, and I do the things I do to try and help women who were abused, for one main reason, Chloe."

"What's the reason?"

"My mother was a victim," I say softly, voice cracking.

She comes to me then.

"How do you mean?" she asks when she's about a foot away. "Did someone hit her too?"

I nod and stare down to where I'm grasping the edge of the mantel. "Someone used to hit her, yes."

"Who? Your dad?"

"No." I shake my head. "My father passed away when I was very young. My stepfather was the one who used to hit my mom. But that bastard pays now every day for what he did to her."

She places her hand on my arm. "What do you mean, Dylan? How does he pay?"

"He's rotting away in prison."

I look at her and see the color has drained from her face.

"W-what happened?" she murmurs.

"He killed my mother, Chloe. He beat her to death."

"Jesus, Dylan…"

"And I was there and saw it all," I go on, unable to stop now that I've started. "I was just a kid at the time, but I swear that some days it feels like it happened yesterday."

She's naturally speechless, until at last she mutters, "Dylan, God, I don't even know what to say."

I wrap my arms around her, holding her close. She doesn't even know it, but I need her comfort so badly.

"You don't have to say anything," I murmur. "This helps, just us holding each other. Besides, words won't change the past."

I lean my cheek against the top of her head and nothing more is said on the subject. There's no need to. We just…are. We're two friends, two broken people, fighting an undeniable attraction. I want more from her, especially now. Finding someone to be so open with, what a fucking gift. I never thought this could happen to me.

It'd be so easy to tip up her chin and kiss her lips. I think she'd be open to it too.

But now is not the time.

I promised Chloe I'd be her friend, and that's what I'm going to do. Even if things do change with us, it can't be too fast. I want to take things slowly with her, proceed with caution. I don't need to damage her heart any further, and I don't care to build something on a shaky foundation.

It'd only collapse.

I pull back, and she smiles up at me sadly.

"Looks like *I'm* the one who ruined our night," I say.

"No." She shakes her head adamantly. "That's not true at all. I think this was good, this sharing. I feel closer to you, Dylan."

I like how she's courageous enough to lay it on the line. Damn, I really want to kiss her right now.

I almost do, but then I remember I'm moving slowly with her.

Shit, I need a distraction.

Gesturing to the kitchen, I say, "Hey, how about we whip up a fresh batch of margaritas. I think we deserve another round."

Chloe laughs and agrees, "We sure do."

We start out sipping our freshly made drinks at the dining room table, but then we move to the sofa where we can relax.

After the heavy talk, we stick to random, unimportant things. Music comes up at one point, and wouldn't you know it, we both like classic rock and old eighties and nineties tunes.

Well, I'm the eighties fan—Chloe is more into the nineties.

Nestling in the crook of the sofa, at the opposite end from me, she nudges my leg with her foot.

Yeah, we lost our shoes hours ago.

"I never pegged you for an eighties fan," she says.

"Ha, you think I'm bad? You should meet my defense partner, Noel. He can name the number one song for every year in the eighties. I'm more of an expert on the one-hit wonders."

"Oh, really now? We'll see about that." She points her empty margarita glass at me. "I'm declaring that the nineties beat the eighties every time, hands down. And to prove it, I can name a one-hit wonder from *my* favorite decade that'll top *any* of your eighties ones."

"Any song, you say?"

"Yes, any song."

"It's on. Hit me with even just *one* good one from the nineties."

"That's easy," she says. "What about 'Steal my Sunshine' from Len? Hello! It's only like one of the best one-hit wonders *ever*."

She hums a few bars, like that'll convince me.

"That song's lame," I scoff. "'Tainted Love' by Soft Cell kicks Len's ass any day."

"No way, and it sure doesn't beat 'Kiss the Rain' by Billie Myers."

"That one is a total girl's song," I counter.

"How can you say that? There's so much heart in it."

"Thank you, you just proved my point."

"Come on, Dylan. You're not even that old. You must like something from the nineties."

I think it over and come up with one. "Okay, there is something from that lame decade that I kind of like."

"Ooh"—she rubs her hands together—"what is it?"

"It's 'Wicked Game' by Chris Isaak."

She rolls her eyes. "Oh, please, like I can't figure out why you chose *that* song. I'm sure the sexy video had nothing to do with it."

"Well, now that you mention it…"

She reaches over and swats my arm. "You're such an ass."

"An ass with good one-hit-wonder taste," I amend.

"Hmm, maybe, but your sexy video song will never top 'Kiss the Rain.' That one stands on its own."

Laughing, I remark, "You really like that song, don't you?"

"I love it," she replies.

"More than 'Steal my Sunshine'?"

"I think so, Dylan."

Since I'm still determined to win our eighties/nineties showdown, I toss out, "What about '867-5309/Jenny' by Tommy Tutone? Everyone loves that one."

"Eh…" She shrugs. "It's not bad. But The Flys' 'Got You (Where I Want You)' would win out over that."

"Hold up," I say, stumped. "I don't think I know that song."

"Whaaat? Hush your face!" She whips out her phone, I assume to cue up the Flys' song I've never heard.

Sure enough, she plays it for me.

"What do you think?" she asks about a minute in.

"It's not bad," I grudgingly admit.

"It sounds even better cranked up." Jumping up from the sofa, she syncs her phone to a wireless Beats Pill she grabs from the other room.

Sitting the Pill down on the coffee table, she says, "Here, listen to it at full blast. It's the best way."

I have to admit, she has me sold.

But I have more for her too.

I take out *my* phone next and sync it. And then I play "You Spin Me Round" by Dead or Alive.

And you know what? I think I win, seeing as we both get up and start dancing all over the place.

"Your neighbors must hate us right about now," I yell over the music as I thumb over to the connecting wall.

"Not likely," she shouts back. "They moved out before I moved in."

"Well, hell." I turn up the volume as loud as it goes, and when "Jump" by Kris Kross starts, we dance and jump and sing along.

I discover that acting like kids makes for great stress relief. Tonight is a testament to that old adage that music soothes the soul. It really does, as I haven't had this much fun in ages.

Chloe even gets me to do the Macarena at one point…and I like it!

But I feel my absolute best when I get her to slow-dance to "True" by Spandau Ballet.

The next song up is Biz Markie's "Just a Friend," and it sure has a lot more meaning than it used to.

Chloe and I are friends, tonight more than ever. I even end up spending the night at her place—on the sofa, of course.

I have to leave early the next morning, though, as practice is at seven.

Needless to say, I'm dead-tired from staying up half the night. But it doesn't matter. My heart is awake and alert.

I don't wake up Chloe before I go, but I do leave her a note, letting her know that I had a really good time and we should do it again "real soon."

After I hang the Post-it to the coffee machine, I program the damn thing so she'll have a fresh cup ready for her at ten sharp. That's when she told me she has to get up for her afternoon shift at the coffee shop.

I head off to practice then, humming one-hit wonders the whole way there.

# 8

## OUCH, MY ASS

### CHLOE

find Dylan's note. His words, and the fact that he took the time to program the machine to have my coffee ready, leave me feeling all warm and fuzzy inside.

I definitely want more from him. But it's not based on just attraction anymore. There's an amazing connection driving us together. It was there from the start, but instead of waning, it's gotten stronger.

I don't think I can fight it much longer.

Maybe though, this is the way it's supposed to work. If only I'd known this before meeting Sten. It was so wrong with us from day one. I sensed it, but ignored all the warning signs. Looking back now with a fresh perspective, I realize it was all too forced with him.

With Dylan, it's not like that at all. Everything is natural and easy.

As I sip my coffee and think things over, I text Dylan to let him know I had an amazing time.

He sends back a text immediately, letting me know that practice just ended. He goes on to mention that there's a game tomorrow night, but he's free in the morning.

*Do you want to do something? We could go grab breakfast.*

*That sounds great,* I type back. *But I have an even better idea.*

*Oh, yeah, do share.*

He's going to love this one… *I want you to teach me how to ice skate.*

*WHAT???? Don't you dare tell me you don't know how to skate! That's blasphemy.*

Even via text, Dylan has the ability to make me laugh.

*Now wait a minute,* I retort. *I lived in Arizona all my life. Ice is hard to come by down there.*

*It's not the early 1900s, babe. There are such things as indoor rinks, you know. Yes, even in Arizona.*

*Ha ha. For your information, I never went to one. So I never learned to skate.*

*We must remedy that. I'll buy you a pair of ladies' skates and block out some ice time for us in the morning at the arena.*

*That sounds perfect. By the way, I'm a size seven.*

*Seven it is, Miss Tettersaw.*

Smiling, I set my phone aside and finish my coffee.

I really do want to learn to skate, and now's the time. I checked this morning and the next step in the X Your Ex program is "Learn to Do Something New." How awesome is it that I'll have the best teacher—a freaking professional hockey player, and a cute one at that.

I just hope I don't fall too much.

"You won't," I state out loud with the utmost confidence. "Dylan will make it so you learn the correct way and stay on your feet the whole time. You probably won't fall once."

*Wrong, wrong, wrong.*

The next morning I discover that even with the most kind and gentle instruction—Dylan is infinitely patient—the ice is unforgiving.

"Ouch, my ass," I mumble when I fall for what feels like the fiftieth time.

Dylan and I are at the arena where the Wolves play. He reserved the ice, as promised, so it's just the two of us.

Thank God, as I wouldn't want strangers, or his teammates, out here watching me slip and slide and flop around on the ice like a fish out of water.

"I'm really out of my element here," I remark as Dylan helps me up.

"No, you're slowly getting the hang of it, Chloe."

This man is *way* too nice.

I shake my head as I hold his arm in an absolute death grip. "I'm definitely a girl from the desert. This ice knows it too. It's intent on taking me down."

Dylan takes my hand and we start skating in tandem.

"Don't feel bad," he says. "The ice takes everyone down when they're just learning."

"Well, it better stop. Or I'm fighting back. I'll go out and grab some sand from the desert and sprinkle it all over. That'll provide some traction."

"Oh, the owners would just love that. I can see the headline now— Girl Ruins Wolves's Playing Surface by Turning it into a Sandbox."

We reach the point where I last fell, and he releases my hand. Since I made it a whole rotation without falling, I ask him if we can go around a few more times. "Stay close, though," I add. "I may need your arm…or your hand."

"You can have any part of me you want, Chloe," he replies.

Is he trying to make me fall for him? If so, it's totally working.

As we begin to skate again, slowly for my sake, I remark, "I bet you never fall anymore."

"I do," he says, laughing. "Sometimes your skate will catch in a weird way, or there'll be a bad spot on the ice."

"*All* of the ice is one giant bad spot, if you ask me."

That makes him chuckle.

I then hit on what must be one of those "bad spots," and I almost do a header. Dylan catches me, though, and keeps me from falling.

"Ugh, that was close," I mutter as I straighten up.

"You're not going fast enough. That's why your skates keep catching. You need to pick up a little speed so you can glide."

"That's easy for you to say."

"Here, let's try it this way."

He turns around so he's skating backward and starts pulling me along.

"I feel like I'm five years old," I state dryly once we're really moving.

"You sure don't look like you're five years old," he replies under his breath.

*Ah, so Dylan has noticed the black leggings and formfitting black performance mock turtleneck I chose for this little outing.*

I may not move like a sexy ninja, but I sure look like one.

"See, you're doing really well now," he says as we begin to soar down the straightaway.

Dylan takes me around the ice several more times. I'm awed that he never seems to tire. And I can't help but think, *with stamina like this, I bet he's amazing in bed.*

Yeah, this friends-only status isn't going to hold much longer.

Too bad we're on the ice. Otherwise, I might just make a move on this hot man.

As it is, I best stick with conversation.

Sighing, I ask, "You don't mind skating backward like this?"

Laughing, he reminds me, "I'm a defenseman. I skate backward most of the game."

"Hmm, good point."

Since I'm enjoying skating now, and I feel like I'm getting it down, I decide to share the X Your Ex program with Dylan.

"Graham got me onto it," I say after explaining the basics.

"It sounds like a fun way to move forward," he notes.

"Yeah, it's fun and lighthearted, but it really helps. 'Learning to Do Something New' is step four."

"Ah, that's why you wanted to learn to skate."

"Pretty much," I confirm.

"So what's the next step?"

"I don't usually peek until a step is completed, but I did page ahead this morning."

"And what is it?"

"Umm…" I'm suddenly wishing I'd not brought this up. "I don't know if I should say."

"Come on, how bad could it be?"

"It's not bad. I just don't know how I'm going to complete it."

"How do you mean? What is it?"

"Uh…"

"Come on, Chloe, tell me. Maybe I can help."

*That's what I'm afraid of*, I think.

And I am. I'm worried Dylan will think I only brought it up

because I want *him* to help me complete the step, which I kind of do.

"Chloe," he prompts.

"Okay, okay. The next step is 'Let Someone Do Something Nice for You.'"

"That doesn't sound so bad. I can definitely help you out with that one."

See, I knew he'd feel obligated.

"Dylan," I begin, taking a breath. "Really, you've done enough. Look at us now. You're teaching me to skate, for heaven's sake."

But he insists, "No, I'm definitely helping. In fact, I already know what I'm going to do that'll be nice."

Curiosity wins out, and I ask, "Okay, what do you have in mind?"

We skate over to the boards for a break. Dylan grabs a bottle of water he left on the edge and takes a drink.

When he hands it to me, I say, "Are you purposely keeping me in suspense?"

"Oh." He laughs. "So that's how it is now. No more 'you've done too much already, Dylan.' I knew you'd cave."

"Oh, stop." I push him, but of course he doesn't budge. "Just tell me."

Finally, he does.

"I'm going to make you dinner, Miss Tettersaw. But I should warn you ahead of time that I'm not the greatest cook in the world. Scrambled eggs are my only real specialty."

"That's fine. Scrambled eggs work for me."

"I think I can do better than that, Chloe."

I'm excited that Dylan's making me dinner, so excited I could just kiss him. Too bad I don't have the nerve.

"Do you want to skate around one more time?" Dylan asks. "I only rented the ice till noon, and it's now ten to."

"Yes," I reply. And since kissing him is still forefront in my mind, and that's going to require us being face-to-face, I ask, "Can we skate like we were doing before?"

"Sure."

Dylan spins around, takes my hands, and starts skating backward.

As we glide along, it's like a clock is ticking. But how can I angle myself to give him a hint? I'm not skilled enough to do anything fancy, like gracefully skate into his arms.

*Damn!*

Seems short of crashing into him, my options are limited.

Still, I decide to give it a try.

I start skating faster. And Dylan, naturally, thinks I'm gaining confidence.

"There you go, Chloe. I knew you had it in you."

Ha, I have a lot more in me than this. Just wait till I end up in his arms. It'll be like a scene from a movie, our own *Ice Castles* moment.

And with that, I propel myself forward.

*Oh, no!*

Instead of skating into Dylan's arms, I crash right into him. It's an *Ice Castles* moment all right. Though it's more like the scene where she wrecks into all the metal chairs than any tender moment one. You know the one, the scene where she freaking blinds herself.

I'm a little blinded myself since my face is pretty much mashed into Dylan's chest. Not that it's bad, but I'm aiming to kiss more than his pecs.

Bravely committed to making this work—damn it!—I toss back my head and twist my body into what I hope is a good kissing position.

Bad move—our skate blades end up tangled.

"Chloe, what the hell are you doing?"

"Oh, oh, shiiiit."

We fall together into a heap. Guess Dylan wasn't lying, he does still fall. But it wasn't bad ice. I, Hurricane Chloe, single-handedly took him out.

Somehow, we get our skates untangled, and Dylan ends up on his back...with me sprawled out on top of him.

*Hmm, not the original plan, but this could work.*

He's so big and warm, so I kind of lie on him.

*I could get used to this, though maybe with fewer clothes. Oh my God, Chloe, get a grip.*

I scramble to sit and end up straddling him. So much for getting a grip.

But I like it. Dylan's chest is so firm beneath my hands. And his heart beats are so strong—*one two, one two.*

Why did I ever think I *needed* to make this happen?

It's going to happen all on its own.

Dylan's gaze burns with want and need, and I'm sure mine does too.

"Dylan," I whisper.

*One two, one two...*

"Chloe..."

*One two, one two...*

It's so quiet in the big arena, just me and him sharing this magical moment.

He places his hands on my hips, and I slide down a little.

*Oooh, he's freaking hard as, well, ice...but so much warmer.*

His hands flex as he rasps, "Sweetheart, what are we doing right now?"

"This," I reply as I lower my mouth to just above his.

He doesn't move; he lets me take the lead.

So I do.

Slanting my head, I boldly touch my lips to his.

*One two, one two…*

His hands wind in my hair, tugging it from my ponytail. *Yes!*

Dylan's knees are up and he's pushing me forward to get me closer to him, to kiss me more fully, like his life depends on it.

I think mine does right now too.

I lose myself in kissing Dylan, and letting him kiss me, until suddenly a male chuckle echoes throughout the arena.

*Who the hell is that?*

"Hey, Culderway." I hear. "What's with sexing it up on the ice, dude? We gotta skate over that same spot tonight, you know."

I lift up from Dylan, breathless and panting.

Meanwhile, he's grumbling, "What the ever-loving fuck?"

"Who is that?" I whisper, too embarrassed to glance over my shoulder to see who just caught us making out and basically dry-humping on the ice.

"It's one of my fucking nosy-ass teammates," he replies loud enough for said teammate to hear.

A chortle sounds out from behind me, and I just have to turn around and see this guy now.

Hmmm, Mr. Voyeur is a good-looking dude with sandy brown hair and a sure-as-shit cocky smirk, one I bet gets him loads of girls. He's casually leaned over the boards, watching our every move with keen interest.

Well, we have been putting on quite a show.

"Which player is that?" I whisper to Dylan, since I have no clue.

Rolling his eyes, he replies, "Jaxon Holland. And he has no room to talk. He's the biggest fucking womanizer on our team."

# 9

# WHEN IT'S RIGHT, IT'S RIGHT

## DYLAN

I don't know if I should thank Jaxon Holland or kick his ass.

I'm leaning toward the latter, seeing as our second-line center has interrupted me and Chloe at, like, the worst fucking possible time. Nonetheless, another part of me feels I should thank him. After all, I did say I planned to move slowly with Chloe, and what we were doing was anything but that.

It was more like a fast track to my bedroom.

*Is that so bad, dumbass?*

*Fuck, I just don't know anymore.*

I never expected Chloe to make the first move. Maybe this means she's ready for more?

I am, that's for sure.

But it's not going to happen on the ice with my cock-blocking teammate looking on.

"Dude, Dylan, you just gonna lay there all day? Some of us are hoping to get a skate in, hopefully without having to dodge bodies rolling around on the ice."

God, he's so annoying. We're not even moving, let alone rolling. I think I'll accidentally check him into the boards next time we're at practice.

Chloe is still sprawled out on top of me, but thank God my hard-on has waned. The last thing I need is for more Jaxon commentary when we stand up.

"Come on, Dylan." Jaxon coughs. "I want to meet your *friend.*"

"Shut the hell up!" I yell over at him.

He's resting his elbows on the boards, smirking over at us.

Sighing, I murmur to Chloe, "I don't think he's leaving anytime soon."

"It would seem not," she replies, rolling her gorgeous blues.

I liked it better when they were filled with lust, not annoyance like now.

Letting her know I'm on the same page, I say, "He has the worst timing."

She touches my cheek. "He does, but it's our fault for making out in public."

"It was fun though, yeah?"

"Very."

"Come on, sweetheart." I sit up with her still safely in my lap. "Let me help you up."

"Thanks," she says.

She steadies herself on my arm, and we stand together.

Motioning to Jaxon, I say, "Let's go over so I can introduce you to

Mr. Bad Timing."

She chuckles, but then whispers she'd hate to fall down in front of my teammate. "Can you help me skate, Dylan?"

"Of course, sweetheart."

Jaxon nods to us as we reach him. "Hey," he says.

Rolling my eyes, I inform him, "The ice is all yours, Peeping Tom."

"Hey, I'm no Peeping Tom. You two were the ones putting on a show." He gestures to where Chloe and I were on the ice and says, "Though I have to say, the surface looks really good over there. Thanks for Zamboni-ing it for me with your bodies."

He laughs, and I murmur, "You are such an ass."

Chloe clears her throat, and I introduce Jaxon and her. She shakes his hand but can't make eye contact. She's clearly embarrassed that he witnessed our hot little make-out session.

Sure enough, she excuses herself after a minute or two of random conversation.

"I need to use the restroom," she says, "Plus, I should get these skates off."

"Do you need any help?" I ask.

"No, I'm good."

Quickly, she plods off on the rubberized runners leading to the locker room.

"Shit, man, I'm sorry," Jaxon says remorsefully once she's out of sight. "I didn't mean to scare her off."

"Your ugly mug would frighten anyone," I retort.

It's just a joke; Jaxon is actually a good-looking guy.

He shoots me the finger and replies, "Fuck off, Culderway."

"Don't get mad. I'm just yanking your chain. You deserve it."

"Yeah, I probably do," he concedes. "But I have to say, I am glad you're finally getting some. Me and the boys were beginning to think you were trying out to be a monk or something."

"Hardly," I scoff. "Just because I'm not a pig like the rest of you animals doesn't mean I've given up sex."

He raises a brow. "So you *are* tapping that?"

"We are so not having this conversation," I warn him.

Even though beneath the bad boy persona there lurks a really good guy, I'm not sharing with Jaxon. Besides, I haven't "tapped" anything yet. I have a feeling, however, based on the way Chloe was grinding on me, that that's about to change real soon.

It won't be meaningless sex, though. I really like Chloe.

Jaxon cocks his head, watching me, and suddenly it hits him. "Fuck me six ways to Sunday, Culderway. This Chloe chick has gotten under your skin, hasn't she?"

I bristle. "First, she's not a 'chick.' She's an amazing woman. And second, no one has 'gotten' to me."

Smug, he retorts, "That's all I needed to hear. You pretty much just confirmed that I'm right."

Ah, fucking hell. He is right. Leave it to Jaxon Holland to make me see the light. I like Chloe far more than I should. She has gotten to me. In fact, she's more than gotten to me. I think I could be falling in love with her.

That's why it's time to take this to the next level.

Chloe changed all the rules when she kissed me. I want to do it again, along with a lot more. I'm not going to be satisfied till I have Chloe under me, screaming out my name.

I need to lay it on the line for her first.

I'm man enough to take a chance and put my heart out there. Let's see how she feels about moving forward. If today were any indication, I'd say she's fully on board.

It's time to make it official—I want Chloe to be my girlfriend.

# 10

## ARTIES OR APHRODISIACS

### CHLOE

The Wolves have back-to-back games following my skating lesson. Dylan is pretty busy, but so am I. I'm working double shifts at the coffeehouse.

The weekend passes with us only texting and talking on the phone. But since he leaves for a couple of road games next week, we make plans to hang out Monday night.

When he calls Monday morning to confirm we're still on, he says, "Damn, I've missed you these past couple of days. This upcoming road trip's going to suck balls."

"For sure," I agree. Sighing, I then add, "What do you want to do tonight?"

Since I'm hoping he picks something mellow, I'm thrilled when he suggests, "Why don't you come over for that dinner I promised you? I have some things I'd like to talk about with you, anyway."

"Uh-oh. It's nothing bad, I hope."

"No way. It's all good, I promise."

He says then that he has to go. There's a lot of noise in the background so it's clear he just finished up with practice.

"Talk to you tonight," I say.

"Yeah, see you then."

We disconnect, and I take a moment to think things over on where we stand. After making out with him on the ice, I think it's safe to assume we're more than friends. And that means tonight is kind of a date.

Because of that, later in the day when I'm debating on what to wear, I choose the cutest dress I own—a tight lacy and white long-sleeved number.

*Hope he's not making anything with a messy sauce.*

If he is, with my luck, I'll get it on the dress.

And then I'll have to take it off.

*Wait. Take it off…*

I am definitely wearing it!

I also choose a white silk bra and panty set. If I do end up taking off the dress—for any reason—I'm making sure Dylan gets an eyeful he won't soon forget.

A couple of hours later, I'm the one getting an eyeful…of Dylan.

He's rocking dark-wash jeans and a red flannel shirt to the $n$th degree. With his tousled dark hair and amazing bod, he could pass for a sexy lumberjack. I can get on board with the lumberjack theme. Maybe Dylan will let me climb him like a tree.

"What do you think?" he says, spinning around to face me.

We're in the middle of him showing me around his nice house, but

I only have eyes for him. Or rather, his tight ass, seeing as it looks so good in denim.

"It's hot," I murmur.

Oh my God, I sound like Paris Hilton circa 2003.

"Thanks," he says, looking confused. "I was actually going for a more rustic look in here. But I guess you could call it 'hot,' if you want."

"Uh, uh…"

I need a cover story, and fast. I don't want him to know I wasn't really paying attention. I scan around the room we're in, some kind of a great room, and realize there's a big stone fireplace with a roaring fire right in front of us.

Gesturing to the flickering flames and crackling logs, I say. "Oh, I just meant it's hot *in here*." I fan myself. "That's some fireplace you have there."

He assures me he won't add any more wood. "It should die down some now," he says as he moves around some of the logs with a poker.

How do I get myself into these messes? I should fess up and tell him I meant *he's* hot. It's not like he'd be offended. But then I realize it is actually kind of warm in here, which is strange since it wasn't earlier.

And now that I think of it—what's that burning smell?

I ask Dylan, and he replies, "I don't smell anything."

I inhale deeply. "No, no, there's definitely something burning. And it's not the fireplace fire."

Just as we're standing here staring at each other, brows furrowed, a smoke alarm goes off.

Dylan says, "Oh, shit."

And I say, "Ow, that's so loud."

I cover my ears when it won't stop. "What's causing that?"

He runs off. "Fuck, it's coming from the kitchen. I think my roast is burning."

"I told you I smelled something!"

I follow him to the ever increasing ear-splitting sound. With both of us coughing—that's how bad the smoke has gotten—Dylan runs in and shuts off the oven.

I want to help—no more helpless girl here—so I squint through the smoke for something I can employ to put out the small fire that's clearly burning in the oven.

And that's when I spy a giant pitcher of water over on the counter.

*Perfect! Firefighter girl to the rescue! If Dylan can be a lumberjack, I can be a firefighter.*

Snatching up the pitcher, I rush over to where Dylan's opening the oven door.

"Get back!" I yell. "I'll take care of this."

"Chloe, wait—"

It's too late. I can't stop from tossing the contents of the pitcher onto the smoldering, though certainly not in flames, roast.

"Better safe than sorry," I say with a shrug.

But then there's a whole new problem. Thanks to my brilliant move, things become smokier than ever in the kitchen.

"That was maybe not the best idea," Dylan coughs out.

"Yeah, maybe not," I dejectedly concur.

I'm actually glad there's so much smoke. I may choke to death, but at least Dylan won't see how mortified I am.

Running around, he flips on a bunch of fans and opens a window. Meanwhile, I work on composing myself. When the room clears, I glance into the oven and notice something lying atop the burned-to-a-crisp roast—one long-stemmed, though now wilted, red rose.

"Oh, shit."

The pitcher I grabbed was a vase!

Not only have I completely ruined Dylan's dinner—the roast may have been salvageable, albeit a tad well-done—but I've succeeded in doing so with a flower no doubt meant for me.

Gesturing to the withered and somewhat charred rose, I say, "I'm guessing that was mine?"

"It was," he confirms.

I start to apologize, but then he says, "Hey, look on the bright side. You used your rose to save us."

I snort. "Ha, all I did was smoke us out."

"It's the thought that counts, Chloe."

He is just too sweet.

"No, I screwed up everything," I whisper, feeling like a fool.

"Stop, this is my fault. I didn't set a timer, nor did I keep an eye on the roast. I think it's safe to say I'm the one who fucked up dinner."

I look inside the oven again. Now that the smoke has cleared, I notice what appear to be little lumps of coal.

"What were those?" I ask.

"Twice-baked potatoes," he replies.

"Aw, roast and potatoes. Sounds like it would've been a nice dinner."

"I should have stuck with scrambled eggs," Dylan murmurs. "It is my signature dish."

I echo his earlier words when I say, "It's the thought that counts, Dylan. Besides, I think we can save this dinner."

He looks at me like I'm crazy, and maybe I am a little, albeit in a good, let's-roll-with-this kind of way.

"I like my roast well-done," I say with a smile.

"Well-done is one thing, Chloe. But this thing is charred to a crisp. It'd be like eating beef jerky."

Always the optimist, I say, "Lumberjacks like beef jerky, I hear."

Dylan's brow furrows. "I don't know what that means, but I think you're wrong anyway. Cowboys are the beef jerky fans. Haven't you ever seen *The Outlaw Josey Wales*?"

"Is that like a spin-off from *Riverdale*?"

"Huh?"

I try to explain. "The only Josie I've ever heard of is Josie and the Pussycats. You know, from the show *Riverdale*."

"I have no idea what you're talking about, Chloe. But you had me at the word 'pussy.'"

"I said 'pussycats,' not 'pussy.'"

"Close enough."

We both lose it then, and I throw a towel at him. "You're impossible, Dylan."

He touches my cheek. "What's impossible is any chance of eating that roast. I think we better just order a pizza."

"Okay," I concede, "sounds good to me."

The pizza is delivered and it's delicious. We devour New York-style slices topped with pepperoni, tomatoes, and artichoke hearts. The artichokes—or arties, as I like to call them—are my call. Dylan's never had arties on a pizza.

"So what do you think?" I ask as he's wolfing down his third slice, one covered in loads of artichoke hearts.

"Fantastic," he mumbles from around the bite.

"See…" I feel smug as I dab my mouth with a napkin. "I told you arties were good on a pizza."

He stops and quirks his brow. "Arties?"

"Yes, arties. I didn't mention it when we ordered, but that's my nickname for artichoke hearts. Graham and I made it up when we were kids, and it just kind of stuck."

"Well, then,"—he holds up another slice—"arties for the win. You were right, they make the pizza."

I love that I can share things like this with Dylan. We can be ourselves when we're together.

I tell him this, and he says, "I like that too." A pause, then, "Can I tell you something, Chloe?"

"Sure."

"You've been really good for me. More than you could ever know."

I have an artie halfway to my mouth, and I freeze.

"How do you mean?" I carefully inquire.

No one has ever told me I've been good for them. Well, no one outside of family. Sten always said the exact opposite, that I caused people nothing but grief, especially him.

Dylan gently pries the artie from my grasp, as I'm pretty much squeezing the thing to death.

He raises it to my mouth, and says softly, "Let me feed you, Chloe, and I'll tell you what I mean when I say that you've been good for me."

I let him feed me, but it's my soul that he fills when he says he's going to share his heart with me.

"I was starting to lose it right before I met you," he says softly. "Things had never gotten that bad for me, and I wasn't sure why. I figured the trigger was when I went to the cemetery to visit my mother's grave back in December. But now I think it all just caught up to me. I came back and I couldn't get a handle on my anger. It was even affecting my play on the ice."

"How so?" I ask.

He takes a deep breath and exhales slowly. "Well, I became so short-fused during games that it was crazy. I was losing my temper all the time. And my concentration was for shit. That just wasn't like me, Chloe. That's why I joined your brother's gym. It was Coach's advice, and I took it. I needed to get myself back on track."

"I understand that," I say, nodding. "That's part of why I started going to Graham's gym too. It helps, doesn't it?"

"It does. But for me, my real turnaround came when I met you. *You* put me back on the right path, Chloe."

I'm stunned. "How in the world did I do that?"

Taking my hand, he says, "I don't know if I can explain, but I'll try. You calm me, even as you excite me. You make me optimistic about the future. That's something I haven't felt in a long, long time. You just give me hope, Chloe."

"Wow," I marvel. "No one's ever said things like that to me, Dylan."

"It's only the truth."

Tears fill my eyes, but not from sadness. For the first time in a long time, I feel truly appreciated.

"So what are we to one another?" I quietly ask.

"We're whatever you want us to be."

"Are you asking me what *I* want?"

"Yes."

"Um, well, I guess I kind of gave it away when I kissed you on the ice, huh?"

I let out a laugh, even as a single tear—one of hope, and disbelief that this man cares for me so much—trails down my cheek.

Dylan brushes it away with his thumb and reminds me, "I kissed you back, remember?"

"You did."

"Chloe, I think you want more, just like I do. So I want us to try to be a couple. I want you to be my girlfriend. Not just my friend who happens to be a girl. What do you say, sweetheart? Are you up for that?"

I laugh. "Are you kidding? More than you could ever imagine."

"Good, 'cause all I want to do right now is kiss the heck out of you."

"Go for it, Dylan."

Closing the gap between us, his lips crash into mine with urgency but with tenderness too.

Soon I want more.

"Dylan," I breathe out.

"Yes, sweetheart," he murmurs as he trails kisses down my neck.

"Take me to bed."

"Shit." He looks up. "I thought you'd never ask."

He carries me up to his bedroom, where he undoes the tie on the front of my dress. Lacy material gapes open, then is quickly whisked away.

I'm on the bed with Dylan above me before I know it. I raise my knee and arch way up. One hand finds purchase at the small of my back while the other frees my breasts from the confines of my bra.

I'm touched and squeezed and plied in all the right ways, and soon I am calling out Dylan's name, begging him for more.

*Make me feel good. Take my pain away.*

I'm desperate. I need him.

I fumble with the buttons on his shirt until I lose patience and just rip the damn thing open.

We laugh as buttons go flying.

"I never really liked that shirt anyway," he tells me.

I run a hand over his rock-hard bicep and say, "But it looked so good on you."

Chuckling, he asks, "Should I put it back on?"

Soaking in his broad shoulders, smooth chest, and the sexy V leading to where I can't wait to go, I reply, "No fucking way."

"That's my girl."

I expect things to continue frenzied, but they don't. For the longest time we just make out, our bodies pressed together, our hearts beating as one. Eventually though, clothes are discarded and just when I think I'll die if he doesn't do something more soon, he reaches down and touches me where I'm slick and wet.

Finding me like that, he groans, "Fuck, Chloe."

"See how much I want you?" I purr.

"I want you just as much, trust me."

I smile up at him. "Let's just see about that."

Reaching down between our bodies, I take him in my hand.

"Oh, wow." He definitely does want me. But what I'm *wow*-ing about is how long and thick he is.

"I can't wait to feel this inside me," I say, squeezing.

That works him up even further, and he rasps, "You better not say things like that or I'm going to take you right now."

*Like that would be a bad thing?*

But Dylan has other plans. He shimmies down my body till his head's between my legs. Then he opens me up with his fingers while he flicks his tongue over my clit.

"Er my God."

"Good, baby?" he asks as he takes a breath.

"Uh-huh."

Chuckling, he gets back to pleasing me. And please me he does.

At some point, we re-adjust our bodies so I can please him with my mouth like he's doing to me.

"God, Chloe, what you're doing feels so good."

I fall apart within minutes, but Dylan somehow holds out. While

I languor in orgasmic bliss, he lays his body back atop mine. But he doesn't enter me. He teases instead, sliding his length along my folds and working my clit with the head of his dick.

I soon shatter once more, this orgasm more prolonged than the first. It's like that one never really ended.

Dylan has me so worked up that he could do anything he wanted to me right now. I am putty in his hands.

But he doesn't take; he only gives, using his body to please me, all without penetrating. It's only when I beg and plead that he finally grabs a condom.

"You sure?" he asks as he rips it open with his teeth.

"I've never been surer of anything in my life," I tell him.

He takes me then, and it's better than amazing.

Afterward, I'm spent and snuggle into Dylan's arms. "I can't believe you have to leave early tomorrow morning for your upcoming road games."

He sighs. "I know. It sucks."

"Ugh, we're going to have to get up *so* early."

"Not you," he replies. He kisses the top of my head. "Go ahead and sleep in. I'll leave a key for you down on the counter. Just lock up when you leave. But again, stay as long as you like."

"Wow," I murmur. "I guess we really are official."

"We are, sweetheart."

This man is amazing, so sweet, so strong, so *good*. I truly feel like with him by my side, nothing will ever go wrong again.

# DICK MEASURING CONTEST IS REALLY NO CONTEST AT ALL

## DYLAN

'm right where I want to be with Chloe. We're finally a couple. And last night? Damn, it was nothing short of incredible.

But now's not the time to be thinking about mind-blowing sex. I'm in the middle of a game, for fuck's sake.

I'm reminded of that fact when someone calls out, "Hey, Culderway, heads up."

That's Brent Oliver. And when he's trying to get your attention, it usually means something good's about to happen. He's the captain of our team for that reason.

Sure enough, here comes the puck.

Brent lobs it onto my stick, and thankfully my reflexes are on-point. I have always had the ability to assess the situation on the ice within milliseconds.

I do that now.

We're down in the opponent's zone, but there's no clear shot to the net due to way too much traffic out in front.

But wait!

Benny Perry is behind the net and no one is on him. I pass him the puck, and he takes advantage of the goalie being focused on the players out in front of the net by executing a beautiful wraparound shot.

Goal!

The guys and I celebrate right in front of the goaltender Benny just burned—ha ha—and then we skate over to the bench.

The game was scoreless, but now it's 1-0 in our favor.

Coach Townsend congratulates us once we're all seated.

"Nice teamwork out there, boys. Keep it up. Five more minutes of play in this period, and then we're on to the third. Stay sharp. We're up by only one goal, and the momentum can change in an instant."

He's right. But it all turns out okay.

We go on to score two more goals in the third period, shutting out our opponents. Our team sure has turned it around from the struggles we faced around the holidays.

There was no cause for celebration then, but there sure is now.

And celebrate we do. The mood is raucous and lively in the locker room. Music is blaring and we're all in high spirits.

Jaxon Holland's sitting next to me, taking off his sweaty gear.

I'm doing the same when he twists to me and says, "Hey, I haven't had the chance to ask, but how are things with you and that girl you were teaching how to skate?" He gives me one of his patented smartass smirks, and adds, "You two engaged yet?"

"Ha ha," I retort.

Looking remorseful, he says, "Shit, I shouldn't have said that.

Seriously, Dylan, how are things going with you two? Her name's Chloe, right?"

Wow, he remembers her name. I think he genuinely wants to know. Still, this is Jaxon, and I can't resist teasing him a little.

"Do you seriously expect me to believe the biggest player on our team is interested in someone's *relationship* status?"

He shrugs. "Eh, what can I say? Maybe I'm going soft in my old age."

"You're like twenty-three, Holland."

"Hey, in some cultures twenty-three is considered ancient."

I roll my eyes. "Not any in the modern era, you ass."

Benny Perry catches that part of our conversation and leans in and says, "I think Holland's referring to the Stone Age."

I make like I'm pondering. "Huh, that would make sense, seeing as Jaxon's pretty much a Neanderthal when it comes to women."

Benny and I bump fists, and Jaxon mutters, "You two are such huge dicks."

"You mean we *have* huge dicks, right?" Benny counters with a laugh.

"Not as huge as mine," Holland volleys back.

Those two, they have nothing on me.

Grabbing my junk, I say, "Hash it out amongst yourselves, boys. 'Cause you already know mine is the biggest of all."

I'm met with jeers and shit being thrown at me.

"You wish, Culderway."

"Bite me."

Ah, I love locker room banter.

The road trip continues with the rest of the games. We win two and lose one.

At this point, there are about two months left in the regular season. We're poised to make a run for the playoffs, and I couldn't be happier.

Not only is my professional life going well, but my personal life is amazing. The worries that weighed me down back in December are long gone.

I have nothing to do but look forward to the future.

Finally!

# 12

# SO IT BEGINS

## CHLOE

I miss Dylan so much.

While he's away, I get a good dose of him by watching the Wolves's games on TV. When we're down to just one before Dylan's set to return to Vegas—and to me!—I invite Graham over for a viewing party.

We haven't hung out for a while, and I've been feeling like a crappy sister. Graham likes hockey a lot so I know he'll be up for it.

I catch him via cell, and he lets me know he'll be at my place by seven, a half hour before the puck's set to drop.

"Perfect," I reply. "But I do have one condition."

"Uh-oh, what's that?"

"Nothing bad," I assure him since he sounds worried. "In fact, I think you'll like this one."

"Go on…"

"I'm up to step six in that X Your Ex program, and this next one is "Live a Little and Eat Stuff that's Bad for You for a Day."

He starts laughing. "Hell, this is right up your alley."

"Hey, what's that supposed to mean?"

Laughing, he says, "It just means I know you love peppermint patties more than life."

"Au contraire, big bro. peppermint patties *are* life."

"I'm guessing that means we're going on a junk food junket tonight?"

"You bet your ass we are."

He informs me he'll supply the candy for my fix. And I, in turn, promise him, "I'll make a bunch of butter-smothered popcorn for you. I know that's your fave fall-off-the-diet-wagon food."

Graham's all about staying at his old playing weight since he hopes to play again. But this night, all bets are off. Candy and popcorn will reign.

We agree it's a plan, and a few short hours later, as we're watching the pregame before the Wolves take on the Vancouver Canucks, Graham and I fully immersed in our bad-for-you pig-out.

"Hey, Chlo, pass me another candy bar."

In addition to my beloved peppermint patties, Graham brought along an assortment of chocolate bar selections.

I hold up a shiny gold and red-wrapped bar and say, "Twix okay?"

"Yep."

Graham and I are lounging on the sofa, and I toss him the Twix.

"I feel like a kid again," he remarks as he rips open the candy wrapper.

"I know, right?" I'm in the middle of stuffing a handful of freshly popped popcorn into my mouth when I add, "Here, haf thome."

My brother makes a face. "Chloe, you are so gross. Dylan might have a whole new opinion of you if he saw you like this—mouth stuffed full, popcorn falling out. It looks like you're waterboarding the stuff."

I laugh, but keep it to myself that Dylan has seen me with my mouth stuffed with something far more, uh, interesting than a handful of popcorn.

"Why are you laughing?" Graham wants to know.

Like I'm going to answer that!

"No reason," I reply, and then I quickly change subjects. "Hey, do you remember how we used to sneak into the Cineplex down the street from where we lived when we were kids?"

He laughs. "Yeah, but there wasn't any 'sneaking' involved. As I recall, that really pretty girl from my high school used to let us in for free all the time."

"I remember her. She was really pretty. And"—I nudge him in the arm—"she had a huge crush on you."

"No, she didn't."

"Yes, she did," I insist. "That's why she never charged us. And for the record, we did still have to sneak…past the ushers."

"Okay, okay," Graham concedes. "But you're wrong about one thing—that girl never had a crush on me. She was just being nice."

I roll my eyes. "You're so clueless sometimes. Like most guys."

"Huh," he murmurs thoughtfully. "You really think she liked me?"

"I *know* she did."

The game starts then, and since the Wolves come out flying, we drop any further teenage-crush talk.

"Those boys must've downed some Red Bull before the game," I remark.

"Yeah, or they inhaled an overload of smelling salts."

I laugh.

It's true, though, that the Wolves are hitting hard and skating fast. Dylan, as always, looks great on defense. My man is blocking shots and keeping the other team from scoring. He and his defense partner, Noel, seem really in sync tonight.

Graham must notice me smiling 'cause he asks, "How are things going with you and Dylan?"

"Great," I reply. "He's a terrific guy, and I really like him a lot."

"I'm glad, Chloe. You deserve someone nice."

We get back to watching the game, which ends in a Wolves victory. *Yay!*

I feel so good in every way, except for maybe my stomach.

"Ow," I lament. "I feel gross."

Graham deadpans, "Gee, I wonder why."

After consuming too much buttered popcorn and candy, I'm paying the price. Still, I declare, "It was worth it. I had so much fun tonight."

"Yeah, I did too," Graham replies. He looks at his watch then. "But I'm afraid the fun will have to end. I need to hit the road. I'm opening the gym extra early tomorrow so a couple of the guys can workout before dawn."

"Ugh, that would never be me," I say.

"No, it wouldn't, sleepyhead."

Ah, my brother knows me so well—I am not, nor ever will be an early riser.

After Graham leaves, I text Dylan to congratulate him on a great game, then I head off to bed.

As I begin to doze off, I begin to think about how my life sure has turned around. Just a few short months ago I was in the process of divorcing Sten. Now that feels like a lifetime ago.

Despite being upbeat about, well, everything, I end up sleeping fitfully throughout the night. That bothers me because I'm intuitive like that. All too often my bad dreams and restlessness are harbingers of a crappy day.

Sure enough, in the morning when I head outside to my car, I discover I have a freaking flat tire.

"Damn it, damn it, damn it!"

I change the tire, a skill taught to me by Graham a long time ago, and then debate if I should still run my errands as planned or head over to the tire store to buy a real tire.

I choose the latter since I hate driving around on those little donut thingies, which is what was in the trunk.

Only problem is payday isn't till tomorrow, and I'm running a little short on funds.

"Hmm, I can always charge it," I muse.

*Ugh, like my cards aren't already maxed-out.*

Suddenly, I have an idea—maybe the flat tire can be patched. If so, it'd save me a ton of money.

At the tire store, the young guy working at the counter is friendly and understanding of my plight.

"Well," he begins, "if the nail is in the tread area, it can probably be plugged. Though I have to warn you, nails in the sidewalls are a whole different story."

"I couldn't really tell where the air was leaking from," I reply. "Not that I looked over the tire all that thoroughly."

"No problem," he says. "Just give me the tire and I'll take it out to the guys in the back. They'll check it over for you."

"Thank you," I say as I hand over the flat tire.

I take a seat in the small customer waiting area and pick up a magazine. I figure I'll be here for a while, but to my surprise, the man returns within minutes.

"Uh-oh, what's wrong?" I ask, standing.

He's holding the flat and looks kind of worried. "Miss," he says, walking over to me, "I'd like to show you something."

"Can the tire not be repaired?"

"I'm afraid not." He lifts the tire and turns it to the side so I can see the damage. Pointing to the sidewall, he says, "Do you see that gash there?"

I look more closely and then I see it.

"Oh my God, how did I miss that?"

There's an absolutely wicked tear about an inch long in the sidewall.

"You probably had the tire turned the other way," he replies. "I didn't see it myself till I got out in the sunlight."

"How could something like that have happened, though?" I inquire worriedly. "I don't recall hitting any curbs or doing anything that would result in *that* sort of damage."

"This isn't from hitting a curb, miss."

Drawing my attention to the tear, he says somberly, "I hate to say it, but it looks like someone purposely slashed your tire."

A chill runs through me. *This was not an accident. Someone intentionally did this.*

The magazine I'm holding drops to the floor. "Who would do this?" I ask, bewildered. "And…why?"

My small neighborhood is home to mainly senior citizens. I rarely even see them. Not to mention, they sure as hell don't strike me as vandalizing types.

I explain all this to the employee and say, "I just can't imagine granny out there slashing tires with a knife."

"I don't know about that either, miss, but someone did this."

Yes, someone did. Was I the target, or was it random? If it was random, then I guess I have bad luck.

But if it wasn't, what does that mean?

Has someone—someone dangerous—taken an unhealthy interest in me?

Suddenly, I just want out of the tire store.

I want to call Graham.

No wait, I'd rather call Dylan.

He makes me feel the safest.

But he's still out of town.

Jeez, could tomorrow just get here already?

# PROTECTING CHLOE

## DYLAN

Fuck, I need to get back to Las Vegas...and fast.

Chloe called this morning, upset as hell. Someone fucking slashed one of her tires.

I'm glad I'm boarding the team jet now.

After we land, I don't bother to stop home first. I drive straight over to Chloe's. When I park my Ferrari next to her Fusion, I check out her tires.

Thank God they all look intact, including the new one she just had put on.

I scan the area.

It's quiet, like always, but I have to wonder—does someone here have it out for Chloe for some reason? She's lived in this small community of homes for only a couple of months. And I know from her telling me that she's had minimal interaction with her neighbors. A hello here and there and maybe the occasional wave, but that's it.

Still, some creep could have her in his sights. These old-timers have young relatives who visit them, after all.

If it is a creeper dude, he's going to be fucking sorry. He picked the wrong girl to mess with. Chloe not only has me to protect her, but she also has Graham.

When I knock on her door, ironically it's Graham who answers.

"Hey, man," I say as he lets me in. "I'm glad you're here."

He nods and assures me, "I wouldn't be anywhere else."

"Me neither."

We shake hands in solidarity then sit down with Chloe in the dining room. I can tell she's shaken up from the way she keeps wringing her hands.

"Hey, it's going to be okay," I try to tell her.

"I hope you're right, Dylan."

"We're going to find out who did this, don't worry."

"Yeah," Graham interjects, "and then we'll take care of the fucker."

"I couldn't agree more," I concur.

Chloe reaches over and squeezes my hand, and then nods to Graham.

"I'm lucky to have you two in my life," she says. "But I've been thinking that maybe it's just a one-time incident and we're all over-reacting. It could've been kids pulling a prank."

"Maybe," I reply. "But I don't think we should operate on that assumption."

"Agreed," Graham chimes in.

We get down then to what is most important—keeping Chloe safe. Graham offers for her to move in with him for a while, but Chloe doesn't like that idea.

I sense her reticence is because of our burgeoning relationship.

That's confirmed when she says, "I think that could get a little uncomfortable, Graham. Dylan and I are dating now and we need time, uh, alone."

Quietly, he murmurs, "I see your point."

I throw out a suggestion of my own then. "What if Chloe moves in with me?"

Graham says, "That's not a bad idea."

Chloe's hesitant, though.

"I don't know," she begins. "The coffee shop is just down the road. And I like living here by myself. I finally have my independence, and I guess I'm just not ready to give it up so quickly."

"I have an alternate idea, then," I reply.

"What's that?" Graham and Chloe say at the exact same time.

Man, you sure can tell these two are related.

Clearing my throat, I say, "I could stay *here* a couple of nights a week. If there's someone watching you, Chloe, seeing me around should make them back off."

"I think that's a fantastic idea," Graham says right away. It's clear he wants his sister safe and protected.

But I've still not heard from Chloe.

"What do you think?" I ask her.

Locking her fingers with mine, she says softly, "I like that plan, Dylan."

"So we're set?"

"Yes."

Jesus, I sure hope this works.

# PART-TIME ROOMIE

## CHLOE

I like the idea of Dylan living with me on a part-time basis. I know he can't just up and move in completely, nor do I think we're ready for that, but *this* I could get used to. Like real fast…

I sigh. Dylan is seated across the table from my brother. He looks so good and strong, as big as Graham, and Graham is huge. One thing for sure, there sure is a lot of testosterone flying around in my little dining room area as we discuss how best to keep me safe.

I sigh again.

Having two protective men in my life makes me feel like one lucky girl. My stalker, if I do in fact have one, stands no chance against these two. And Dylan will be staying with me now. I can't imagine a vandalizing kid *or* a crazy-ass adult male will dare mess with me with Dylan around. He's intimidating, big and strong, and in optimum shape.

Yeah, I'll be just fine.

And I'm going to make the most of Dylan staying with me, even if it is only a couple of nights a week.

We wrap up and Graham leaves. Dylan does as well so he can go pack up some of his belongings. I'm excited he's staying the night.

When he returns a short while later, with a couple of bags in tow along with some hockey sticks, I tell him to put his things anywhere he likes.

He heads straight for the spare bedroom and oh my God, my heart melts. Even though we've slept together, how cute is it that he doesn't want to assume anything?

Still, I have a feeling he'll be in my bedroom soon enough. Lord knows I'm ready for a repeat of our night at his house.

Oh, but I can play the unassuming role too. In fact, that evening I decide to have a little fun with it.

When Dylan emerges from the spare bedroom, I nonchalantly ask, "Are you hungry? You must be, right? All that packing and running around today probably has worked up your appetite."

Crossing his arms over his wide chest, he mulls it over.

"Yeah, I probably could go for a bite."

"Perfect." I stand. "I'll get to work on a nice salad."

Dylan grabs two hockey sticks that are leaning against the living room wall and the muscles in his arms flex and bulge.

*Gah!*

"I'm good with a salad," he says. "But I think I'll need something a little more substantial than just some lettuce leaves."

"I bet you do," I murmur.

All his ripped and tight muscles surely require lots of nutrients to keep them so hard and strong. I'm so busy admiring Dylan's physique that I don't realize he's in the middle of asking me something. So much for playing it coy.

"What was that?" I say. "I was, uh, just daydreaming there for a sec."

*Yeah, daydreaming about you and your muscles and how soon I can get under them again.*

"I could tell," he murmurs.

His accompanying smirk leaves no doubt that he knows I was drooling over him.

But he lets it slide, instead saying, "I was just asking if you have any chicken breasts handy? Either breasts or thighs would work."

*I have some breasts and thighs for you,* I think to myself.

Out loud, I just say, "Uh-huh, I have both in the fridge."

Clearly, I need to get laid…by Dylan…again…and soon.

"Okay, good," he says as he slips the hockey sticks into the spare room, his voice fading and then becoming clear again when he steps out into the living room. "I noticed before that you have a grill out back, so I was thinking I'll grill us up some chicken to go with the salad."

"That sounds delicious, but…"

"What, Chloe?"

Based on his last attempt at cooking, I can't help but blurt out, "I don't know if grilling is a good idea."

He looks perplexed. "Why's that?"

"For starters, property management wouldn't appreciate you burning down this unit. Face it, Dylan, you're a dangerous chef."

"Ouch!" He places his hand over his heart like I just mortally wounded him. "That's low, Chloe."

He sounds serious, but his sneaky smile gives him away. Still, he maintains, "Poking fun at my noble attempt, albeit botched, to make you a delicious roast is just plain wrong."

"No," I counter, playing along, "what you did to that roast was just plain wrong, Dylan."

"Wow, who knew sweet Chloe Tettersaw could be so cruel. I'm shocked."

Uh-oh, is he kidding, or is he serious?

I can't tell.

*Crap, I've taken things too far.*

Fearful I've upset him, I blurt out an apology.

"I'm sorry. Really I am. I was just joking, Dylan, I promise."

He comes over to me. "Hey, hey, I know that. There's no need to apologize. We were just having fun."

Peering up into his deep brown eyes, I whisper, "You're not mad at me, then?"

"Hell no."

"And I didn't hurt your feelings?"

"Fuck no. You should hear the shit the guys say to each other in the locker room."

"Thank God." I breathe a sigh of relief, and he puts his arm around me. "I'm glad to hear that. I thought maybe I'd gone too far."

He turns me so I'm facing him. With his hands on my shoulders, he looks at me like he's trying to figure something out.

After a beat, he asks, "Did someone once tell you that? Like when you were joking about something?"

"Uh-huh." I nod once. "Sten used to say crap all the time when I tried to tease him."

Shaking his head, Dylan murmurs, "What an asshole."

I don't want to keep things from him ever, but it doesn't make sharing any easier.

Stepping back, I cross my arms. "It was like that for a long time, so long that it became the new normal."

"Chloe," he sighs.

"I know that's really fucked up. And I'm embarrassed I put up with it."

"Hey, don't do that to yourself; Sten guilt-tripped you enough. The important part is that you left...while you still could."

I know Dylan's referring to his mom. She didn't leave and it ended as badly as it could. I shudder at the thought that that could've been me.

Dylan takes me in his arms. "Hey, let's talk about something else, okay?"

We focus on fixing dinner from that point on and spend the next half hour getting all the ingredients together. Since I want to keep moving forward—that fucking bastard Sten will never win—I go ahead and start teasing Dylan again about roast night.

"I better make sure all the smoke detectors are in good working order," I say when he has all the chicken prepped.

"Won't matter," he snarks back. "I'm cooking these outside on the grill, remember?"

"Ha, there was a lot of smoke last time, as I recall. A repeat of that and the sprinklers will go off."

"You're relentless," he tells me.

And this time I reply with, "You bet your ass I am."

No cringing, no stress. *So this is what a healthy relationship looks like. I could get used to this.*

As it turns out, Dylan doesn't burn the place down, and no sprinklers or smoke detectors go off.

"See, you can trust me," he says as he brings in perfectly grilled chicken.

"I do trust you, Dylan."

Our eyes meet, and he knows I'm talking about far more than chicken.

After dinner, we decide to watch a movie. But we need to get comfortable first. I go to my bedroom and throw on my favorite flannel pajamas, the ones with little rose bouquets all over them.

I pass a mirror on my way out and falter.

"Wait, this is no good. What the hell are you thinking?"

If my goal is to get Dylan back into bed, and it is, it's probably best not to have him thinking he's rooming with a granny.

*Perish the thought!*

PJ's go flying into the night, and my sexiest camisole and shortest boy shorts come out.

I go from grandma to pinup in less than sixty seconds.

*Let's see how long Dylan can resist me in this.*

I make it back out to the living room before he does. But just as I'm getting settled on the sofa, he emerges from the spare bedroom, wearing black lounge pants and a tight white performance shirt that clings to his sculpted muscles in all the right ways.

When he sees me, he stops in his tracks. "Wow, Chloe."

Hmm, I seem to have gotten my "I'm ready for some sexing" message across with my skimpy attire.

*Yes! This girl is getting some hot hockey ass tonight!*

Dylan, trying to play it cool, crosses his arms over his broad chest and asks, "So what do you want to watch, Chloe?"

I pat the spot next to me and say huskily, "Does it really matter?"

# 15

## VOYEUR BUNNY

### DYLAN

Chloe's right, it doesn't matter what we watch. With the way she looks in those sexy red boy shorts and pink camisole, TV is the last thing I have in mind.

So the flat-screen remains dark.

We make out on the sofa for a while like a couple of horny teens until I suggest, "Let's move this to the bedroom."

"We should go to mine," she says. "It's bigger."

We're naked in no time once we're on the bed.

Chloe rises to her knees and begins kissing down over my abs, lower, lower…

"What are you doing?" I rasp, like I don't know and don't love every minute of it.

"This," she replies, looking up at me and smiling coyly before she takes me in her mouth.

"Fuck, that's good," I murmur as she sucks and licks and drives me to the edge.

But I don't want this over yet.

Nudging her, I indicate that she should stop. When she does, I flip her over on to her back.

"It's your turn now, beautiful," I say.

Shimmying down between her thighs, I touch my tongue to her clit. "Ah, Dylan," she moans.

"More?" I ask, teasing her.

"Yes, more!"

It doesn't take long to get her to where she needs to be.

"Let go," I urge when I feel her tensing, trying to hold back. "Trust me, Chloe."

That does it. She lets go completely, grinding into my face. When I insert a finger, she comes apart, calling out my name.

Sexy times grind to a halt though when we both hear a weird scuffling noise outside her window.

"What the fuck was that?" I murmur, rocking back onto my heels.

"I have no idea," Chloe whispers.

She sits up quickly, and though the blinds are tightly drawn, she pulls the sheet up around her.

Immediately, I go into protective mode.

*Fuck this. I am not having her feeling frightened in her own home. This is why I'm here, right?*

"Damn straight it is," I mumble as I jump out of bed and throw on my discarded lounge pants.

"What are you doing?" Chloe asks.

"I'm going outside to check on things."

"Oh, Dylan, be careful."

I assure her I will before I leave.

It's strange out behind her unit, though. Everything looks fine. There's no one around, and nothing appears disturbed or out of place. Not that anyone would loaf around back here, seeing as there are sharp cacti and scraggly bushes just about everywhere. Certainly this is enough underbrush to discourage a random creeper, right?

*But maybe not*, I think when I hear the scuffling noise again.

"You're not getting away this time," I growl as I swing my phone in the direction of the sound.

"What the…?" I start laughing. "Shit, no way."

A cute jackrabbit is frozen in the light from my phone. Once his wits return, he scurries away, but not before I snap a pic of our little Peeping Tom.

Back in the bedroom, I pass the phone over to Chloe. "I think I found our voyeur. He's a little furrier than I expected, though."

When she looks down, she cracks up. "Aw, I love this pic. What an adorable little fellow. I feel bad we were thinking it was a weirdo trying to sneak a peek."

"He could still be a weirdo, Chlo," I joke as I try not to laugh. "Maybe even a pervert bunny."

She throws a pillow at me, but I catch it easily.

And then I crawl back to where I want to be—in her arms.

Trailing my nose along her neck, I whisper, "Now, where were we?"

# 16

# PURPLE RAIN

## CHLOE

The next day, Dylan has to leave early for a flight to an away game up in Edmonton.

Even though I'm barely conscious, I'm comforted by the gentle kiss he brushes across on my cheek, as well as the sweet goodbye he murmurs in my ear.

"I hate that you have to leave," I whisper as I rouse to life.

"It won't be long, sweetheart. I'll be back tomorrow."

Even though it's only slightly more than twenty-four hours that we'll be apart, I still dread it.

I fall back asleep after Dylan leaves, but wake again to the sound of the alarm buzzing. I have a shift at the coffee shop that begins at noon.

As I get ready for the day, I can't help but think about last night with Dylan. Every part of me tingles at the memory of all we did. He's such an amazing man, as thoughtful and caring in bed as he is out of it.

The stuff we did before the bunny interrupted was fun, but the hot sex afterward was even more amazing. The first round was fast and hard, but the second was gentle and loving.

*Whoa, "loving"? Where did that come from? Does Dylan love me? Jeez, I don't know. And wait, do I love him?*

If I'm honest with myself, I think I'm starting to fall. No, I *know* I am. Shit, I'm falling for Dylan Culderway.

But is that such a surprise?

No. He makes me feel safe and protected, and he's a kind man with a good heart.

Yeah, I'm good with this. It's okay to love again. I guess I really am healing.

My day at the coffee shop flies by. Maybe that's because I feel happier than I have in a long time. Now that I've accepted I am falling in love with Dylan, it's like I'm at peace. I can't wait to tell him too.

But eek, I hope he loves me back. If my instincts are correct, he does.

My shift ends in the evening, and as I'm walking back to my place the sun is setting, drenching the sky in shades of orange and violet.

*It's so pretty.*

Way off in the distance there's a dark purple cloud with—I squint— rain coming out of it.

Wow, that's something I've never seen. It's like purple rain, for real. Maybe Prince saw something like this long ago and it became the inspiration for his hit song.

Well, whether it was or wasn't, the purple rain is inspiration for me.

I decide then and there to do something I've wanted to do for a long time—change my hair by adding in some colorful highlights.

The next step in the X Your Ex program is "Make a Change," so this is perfect. Two birds, one stone, and all that.

*That's it, I'm doing it!*

I detour to a strip mall where there's a hair salon. The stylist there informs me what I want to do is called a "dip dye."

"Do you know what color you'd like?" she asks me.

"That's an easy one." I think about the cloud with the rain and say, "I want purple."

"Purple it is, then," she says with a smile.

When she's finished, she blow-dries my hair, and then tells me to check out the results.

"Oh my God, I love it!" I exclaim as I peer into the mirror.

I do too. In fact, I love my new look so much that I text Dylan a selfie. It's close to game time, though, so I'm not sure he'll see it right away.

But lo and behold, he does and texts back, *Gorgeous shade. You look beautiful, babe.*

*Thanks,* I respond. *I know it's almost game time, so we can talk more later on. Go kick some ass for now!*

*Thanks, Chloe. We will.*

I flip on the game the second I'm home. Dylan skates circles, sometimes literally, around his opponents. Tonight he's also blocking shots and throwing punishing checks.

*That's my guy.*

The Wolves win the game, and I go to bed feeling fantastic.

Sadly, my soaring feeling starts to wane the minute I'm awoken by another weird noise.

*Not again. And not when I'm alone. Crap.*

It's a little after three in the morning, and this time there's not just scuffling but some sort of scraping sound as well.

I try to convince myself it's probably voyeur bunny scratching at something.

But I need to be sure or I'll be up all night.

Jumping out of bed, I throw on a robe. And phone in my hand, so I can call 911 if need be, I tiptoe over to the window.

I'm not brave enough to raise the blinds. I mean, what if some creeper *is* out there?

"I'm sure it's just your bunny friend paying you a visit," I try to assure myself.

But bunny friend or not, I open the blinds only a crack.

No one is outside my window, thank heavens. No bunny, no person, nothing.

"You were probably imagining the whole thing," I murmur. "Maybe it was a dream."

I sleep soundly after that. There are no more strange noises waking me up, and I feel better about things the next day.

Once I'm dressed, I decide to do a little investigating on my own, just to satisfy my curiosity and put to rest any lingering concerns. I'm so confident that I'll find nothing out by my window that I even grab a few carrots from the fridge, just in case voyeur bunny does show up again.

But as I'm placing the carrots by the base of a large cactus just outside my window, I'm stopped cold.

"What the hell?"

Directly beneath the windowsill are two fresh cigarette butts. Shit, bunnies don't smoke. But people do. *Fuck.*

I glance around nervously. It's daytime, so no unsavory characters are lurking, of course.

But this confirms my worst fear—someone *was* outside my window last night. They were clearly smoking and probably trying to see in, just like the other night.

I shudder, wondering if this is also the same weirdo who slashed my tire.

Holy hell, the stalker scenario is looking more and more likely.

But who the hell would stalk me?

My first thought is Sten. But he doesn't smoke. I really don't know anyone who does. Not that I know that many people here in Vegas.

So shit, who the hell is after me?

And more importantly—why?

# 17

## MOVING IN

### DYLAN

When Chloe tells me about the cigarette butts, I do two things. One, I have a surveillance camera installed outside her bedroom window. And two, I put a stop to me staying at her place only a few nights a week.

That's right, once I return to town, I move in with her full time.

I also transfer my things from the spare room to her bedroom.

"It's silly to keep your things in there when we sleep together every night," she says.

"Babe…" I kiss her cheek. "I couldn't agree more. You don't have to convince me."

There's a moment then, where she just kind of looks up at me.

*Tell her you love her, you fool,* an inner voice screams.

I mean, I do. Love her, that is. Chloe Tettersaw owns my heart.

I open my mouth to say the words, but her damn cell phone rings and blows the moment.

She answers and puts the phone on speaker since it's a call from Graham.

He's making sure I made it back to town and there's no need for him to sleep over tonight.

"No, I'm good," she tells her brother. "Dylan's here with me now."

"Hey, man," I call out.

"Hey, Dylan, good game last night."

"Thanks, Graham."

I feel like Chloe's well-protected with me and Graham by her side. But I do have a lingering concern. The only place I can't protect her is at the coffee shop.

I bring this up to Chloe once we disconnect with Graham.

She listens intently, but assures me there are lots of employees around when she's working.

"What about when you leave?" I ask. "You walk home, right?"

"I do most of the time, yeah."

Sighing heavily, I say, "Maybe that's not such a good idea for a while. You should drive to and from work until we know what's going on."

"Ugh, Dylan."

Sitting down on the sofa, she places her head in her hands. "I hate this," she says, her voice muffled. "I'm finally independent and bam!" She looks up. "I'm going backward."

I sit down next to her. "Sweetheart, you can't look at it like that. You're just being cautious."

Leaning back, she blows out a breath. "Yeah, but it sucks that I can't walk to work anymore. I enjoy that time to think."

I come up with an idea. "I think there's a compromise, Chlo."

Running her hand through the soft curls of her long hair, she says, "Hit me with it, Dylan, 'cause I'm out of ideas on my own."

"You could drive when you have an evening shift, but still walk to work for your day shifts."

It's a fair concession. There's lots of traffic along Chloe's route, so as long as it's daytime she should have no problems.

Still, I feel compelled to add, "I'm buying you a pepper spray, though."

Chloe loves the walking-in-the-day-only compromise, and she's good with the pepper spray too.

Once we switch over to lighter topics, I ask her, "Would you want to come to tonight's game? Brent Oliver's fiancée, Aubrey, has an extra ticket that's in the wives and family section. Her sister, Lainey, isn't attending because Nolan is still hurt and out of the lineup."

Chloe looks super excited, but then her face falls.

"I like the idea," she says. "But I don't know."

"You won't be sitting alone," I assure her. "Aubrey will be with you. The two seats are together. She's really nice, Chloe, you'll like her."

Sitting all alone at a game isn't Chloe's idea of a good time. In the past, I've offered her tickets, but she always declines, citing that she would go if she had a friend to sit with.

Hey, I don't blame her. The games are much more fun when you're with someone.

"There's a bonus," I say. "Not only will Aubrey sit with you, but she knows the game in and out. Brent's made sure of that."

"Hmm, maybe I should go," she says.

I can tell she's warming to the idea, and I utter encouragingly, "You'd have a lot of fun, Chloe."

She gives me a yes answer, so I text Brent to have Aubrey hold the ticket for Chloe.

"You can drive to the arena with me," I say. "I'll also have Brent tell Aubrey to meet you outside the section you'll be sitting in."

She nods demurely, but Chloe can't fool me. She's more excited than she's letting on.

Sure enough, on the way to the arena, her leg is bouncing and she's humming along to a song on the radio.

When the tune ends, I turn down the volume and remark, "You're sure in a good mood."

"I'm happy to finally be going to one of your games. So, of course, I'm excited."

"You're going to have so much fun, Chlo."

"Yeah, I think so. I haven't been to a game in so long."

"Why is that?" I ask, knowing she was a hockey fan long before she met me. "I would've thought you'd have gone to a bunch of Coyotes games while living in Phoenix."

Quietly, she says, "Sten didn't really like hockey. I went to games with Graham when he lived there, but then he moved up here."

"I'm despising this Sten the more I hear about him," I grumble.

"He is pretty despicable," she agrees.

I sigh. "I hate to ask, Chloe, but are you sure that dick isn't the person we should be looking at?"

"You really think Sten could be my stalker?"

I wince. I hate that word because I hate that she may really have one. I'm secretly hoping the slashed tire and the noises and cigarette butts outside her window all turn out to be random, unrelated incidents. But, let's face it, they're probably not.

"He seems the most likely candidate," I grimly reply.

Chloe, though, insists, "No, I don't think so. Sten lives in Arizona. Plus, he was never a smoker."

I sigh, reluctantly conceding, "Yeah, you're probably right."

I'm not fully convinced, however, so after I drop Chloe off outside her gate, I drive to the players' parking area and proceed to call a private investigator I know personally from my involvement with victim advocacy and law enforcement.

We make small talk for a minute then I fill him in on the situation.

"Can you check out this Sten guy?" I ask. "I want to be 100 percent sure he's not anywhere near the Las Vegas area. If he is, well…I don't even want to think about it."

"I'll check it out," my PI says. "But if he's in Arizona, it's probably not him."

I don't know if that's good or bad.

If not him, then *who* is stalking Chloe?

# 18

# THE GAME IS AWESOME AND SO IS AUBREY

## CHLOE

Outside the arena, Dylan pulls up to the curb at the gate I need to go in. Before I leave, I give him a hot-as-hell kiss, and then, still embraced, I wish him good luck in the game.

"Mmm," he murmurs as we reluctantly separate, "maybe I should blow the game off so we can go home and continue this."

I playfully smack him in the arm. "Stop. You know you can't miss a game for no good reason."

"I'd say taking you home to sex you up would be an *excellent* reason."

I can't disagree, but my conscience compels me to remind him, "Your team needs you."

I pop open the door, but before I get out, I promise, "We'll have fun later."

Inside, I find Aubrey Shelburne, Brent Oliver's fiancée, rather easily. She's hard to miss, stunning woman that she is. I feel intimidated as I walk up to introduce myself. But then she turns around, and her pretty turquoise eyes hold nothing but kindness and warmth as she recognizes me.

I know then that everything Dylan has told me is true—I'm going to have a great time tonight.

Sure enough, Aubrey and I hit it off like old friends.

"It's good to finally meet you," she says warmly. "I've heard so many nice things about you. And Brent showed me a picture of you and Dylan, and you sure can tell that man's into you."

"Aw, I care for him quite a bit too," I softly reply.

Aubrey goes on to say, "You know, Dylan's such a private person. And he's never been a casual dater. That's why all of us know you're someone special to him."

Wow, Dylan and I do care deeply for one another, but to hear it confirmed makes me feel amazing.

"That makes me feel so good to hear," I share with Aubrey. "And I'm so glad I came tonight."

Aubrey and I talk some more outside our section, but when it's announced that there's only a minute left till game time, she remarks, "Yikes, we better get to our seats."

It's cool that we lost track of time. That means I really like Brent Oliver's fiancée. She's not snooty or bitchy in the least.

As we make our way to our seats—me proudly wearing my #27 Culderway jersey, and Aubrey in Oliver #51—I mention that Brent's number is cool to have out here in the Nevada desert.

"You know, because of Area 51," I clarify.

Aubrey bursts out laughing, though I have no idea why.

We find our seats and once we're settled, I ask her why Area 51 is so funny.

She cryptically replies, "Oh, dear little Chloe, you don't know the half of it."

Hmm, with the way she's smiling, I absolutely need the details of this inside joke.

But first there's a game to watch.

The puck drops, and the Wolves dominate from the start. Brent is on fire, and Dylan is playing well too. The defensive pairing of him and Noel, his usual partner, are on the ice with Brent's top line throughout most of the game. That makes it nice 'cause Aubrey and I can root for our guys together.

"Our boys are looking good," she says when a Wolves power play begins.

"They sure are," I agree.

"Get a goal, get a goal," Aubrey chants under her breath when a two-on-one breaks out.

It works!

Brent scores when Dylan puts the puck on his stick.

*Yes!*

Aubrey and I jump up out of our seats, erupting in cheers and hugs.

During the second intermission, I ask her, "So how'd you meet Brent?"

She raises a brow. "You've never heard the story?"

I shake my head.

"Well, it's a good one," she says.

Aubrey goes on to tell me how she came on board last season with the Wolves when the team hired her as Brent's life coach.

"After a *very* awkward first meeting," she adds with a grin.

"You didn't like each other at first?" I ask.

"Ha, that's putting it mildly."

"But you fell in love somewhere along the line."

"Yes, we sure did. And now we're getting married."

"This summer, right?"

"Uh-huh. You'll have to come, Chloe, with Dylan as your date."

"Of course we'll be there," I promise, before I dreamily add, "Happy endings are the best."

Nudging me, Aubrey says, "They are. And I bet you get yours with Dylan."

"Maybe," I murmur. "I hope so."

"You will," she says with certainty.

If someone had told me six months ago that this is where I'd be today, I never would've believed it. I have Dylan in my life, and I'm in love with him. I live in the same city as my brother once again, and, more importantly, I'm finally living the life I always wanted.

Plus, bonus—I look over at Aubrey—I have a new friend.

# LOVE BUBBLE

## DYLAN

Wow, Chloe's all over me once we return to her place. Not that I'm complaining. I just need to catch up.

She was quiet on the ride back, so I chalked it up to her thinking about the game and her time with Aubrey. She told me when she first got in the car that they hit it off really well and plan to do something again soon.

Enough about Aubrey, though—Chloe's seduction of me just swung into full gear.

"Let's move this to somewhere more comfortable," she says softly as she's stroking me through my pants.

I grunt out a husky "Hell, yeah" and start backing her toward the bedroom.

But seeing as I'm already hard as fuck, getting there at this slow pace is unacceptable.

I pick Chloe up, carry her in, and toss her onto the bed.

"Dylan," she purrs as she props up on her elbows. "Feisty. I like it."

"Oh, I'll show you feisty, woman."

I stalk toward her and she squeals in what sounds like delight.

Good. I'm on her in ten seconds flat, and from there it's a blur of clothes flying this way and that. I can't tell what is hers and what is mine, or who exactly is removing what.

But who the fuck cares?

Getting skin-to-skin as soon as possible is the goal.

When we finally are just that, I hover over Chloe and say, "You're beautiful, sweetheart. You know that, right?"

Reaching up, she caresses my stubbled cheek. "Dylan, you're always so sweet to me. I just hope I'm as good to you."

"You are, Chloe. You make me feel so loved."

*Shit, that just slipped out.*

"Uh, uh, what I meant to say was—"

"Dylan, stop." She smiles up at me. "It's okay to say you feel loved, because you *are* loved."

*I must be dreaming.*

To make sure I'm not, I ask, "Are you saying what I think you are?"

"Yes. I love you, Dylan Culderway."

And with that, so many wounds on my soul are healed. Her words have stitched them up, a testament to the power of true love.

"God, I love you too," I breathe out.

It's true. I love her so much it hurts…but in the best kind of way.

"I want you," she says, parting her legs. "Take me, Dylan, right now."

There's no reason not to slip into her, not anymore. We've had "the talk" more than once and we're good in all ways. Shit, even our love for one another has been declared.

So I pierce her unsheathed. And fuck me all to hell. This is good, *too* good. I have to pull out some.

Chloe whimpers, "No. Give it all to me, Dylan. I need *all* of you."

Fuck it. With one smooth, fluid thrust, I'm once again engulfed in her silky warmth. And guess what? I don't come undone after all. I love her slowly and steadily, staving off the inevitable.

But the inevitable still does, of course, come…for both of us.

We're not anywhere done, though. We can't get enough of each other, not this night. So Chloe and I do it over and over again, till we pretty much can't anymore.

"Gah, that was amazing," she says as we lie in each other's arms after round who-the-hell-knows.

I chuckle. "Shit, you're going to be so sore tomorrow. At this rate, I will be too."

"Good. I don't know about you, but I want to be reminded of this all day tomorrow. In fact…" She raises a brow. "Do you want to go for one more round?"

"Hell, I'm game if you are."

I feel like I'm in a bubble, a love bubble.

If only we could stay here forever.

# 20

# THUMPER

## CHLOE

I open the X Your Ex program and find step number eight is "Open Your Heart."

Talk about perfect timing!

I'm already there—I opened my heart to Dylan last night.

Seems I'm healing and moving forward, even without the prompts in the pamphlet.

Guess I'm stronger than I realized.

Still, it amazes me. For a girl who felt so closed off from love—and life, in some ways—I jumped back in and actually won.

In fact, I'm kicking ass. What I have with Dylan is pure and genuine. It makes me mad I ever wasted any time on Sten.

That was the past, though, when I was blind.

My eyes are open now.

I'm freaking awake, baby!

The next few days are amazing. Dylan has all home games so we immerse ourselves in playing house. My stalker, or whatever weirdo was spying on me, seems to have disappeared.

Who knows what brought about this welcome change?

Maybe the camera Dylan had installed is actually working and keeping the creep deterred. There's been no recording of anyone out back, save for some very cute clips of our voyeur bunny friend.

Ever since Dylan and I reviewed that footage, amid a slew of chuckles from him and ooh-ing and aww-ing from me, we've been debating over whether our furry friend is a jackrabbit or a domestic bunny.

At an impasse, today I demand we watch the tape one more time.

"To settle this once and for all," I say.

After another viewing of the rabbit hopping around and munching on carrots I now feed him on a regular basis, we still can't agree.

"It's domesticated, for sure," I state. "Look at how he loves those carrots."

"A wild rabbit would eat them too, Chloe. It's food, right?"

"Yeah, but look at how plump this bunny is. I know the coloring is the same, but aren't jackrabbits all sleek and fast?"

Dylan thinks it over. "Maybe, but how would a domestic rabbit end up here?"

"Very easily." I wave my hand toward the empty unit next to mine. "Whoever lived next door probably abandoned the poor thing."

"Nah, I think it's a wild rabbit, babe."

"Well, in any case, we should name him."

"I thought he already had a name. You call him Voyeur Bunny all the time."

"That's not exactly accurate, though. He just hangs out back there and eats. I think he deserves a more appropriate name."

"What are you thinking?" Dylan says. "I know you must have something in mind."

I giggle, 'cause I sure do. "What about Thumper?"

Laughing, he says, "If that rabbit was peeking in at us this morning, that's probably the name he has for me."

"You have a point," I say.

And he does. Dylan was *very* enthusiastic when we were sexing it up earlier.

"Maybe we better think of a different name for him."

"I think so," Dylan agrees.

We decide on "Jack," since a certain someone is so damn sure our rabbit is a jackrabbit.

"It's not the most imaginative name," I lament, "but it'll do."

"Good, so that's done." Dylan stands. "Everyone has a name."

Eyeing him mischievously, I look up at him and reply. "Yes, everyone does. But you're no longer Dylan. From this day forward, I'm going to call you Thumper."

"Not in public you aren't!"

"Yes, I am," I insist as I jump up and prepare to run. "And there's nothing you can do to stop me."

"Oh, yes there is."

Dylan grabs me up in his arms and right there on the living room sofa, he lives up to his new nickname, "thumping" the hell out of me as he makes me promise to keep my pet name for him strictly between us.

I'm willing to agree to anything now, so I pant, "Yes, yes, of course, Thumper."

That makes him give it to me even harder, which was really my goal.

Everything is so good and happy with us that I hate it when Dylan has to leave for back-to-back road games.

The good news is I'm no longer scared to be alone.

"I have Jack here with me," I tell him on the day he has to fly out. "And we're a duo no one dare cross."

"Yeah, sure, babe, whatever you say."

Dylan goes on to tell me that all the "thumping" he's been giving me must be messing with my head.

"Then mess away," I say.

But Dylan's all in serious-mode. "Babe, before I leave we really need to go over safety precautions."

"Ugh, okay. Let me see… I need to diligently lock all the doors and windows *and* make sure the camera is always on."

"That's right."

Dylan looks at me and frowns, and I say, "What now?"

"Are you sure you don't want Graham to stay with you while I'm gone?"

I roll my eyes. "I don't need my brother staying here. I told you I'll be fine."

"Okay, but promise once more that you'll double-check everything we just went over."

"I'll do you one better," I proclaim. "I promise to *triple*-check everything."

"Perfect," Dylan says, sounding relieved. "Now get over here and kiss me goodbye, woman."

I gladly do and kiss him till I'm dizzy.

The next day, as I'm on my way out the door to meet up with Aubrey for dinner, I do as I promised Dylan—I triple-check all the locks *and* make sure the camera is on.

I drive to the bar and grill we decided on so that we can watch our guys take on the Dallas Stars. When we made the arrangements, Aubrey informed me she has a present for me.

"It's something every player's girlfriend or wife *must* have," she said. "In fact, I've made it my personal mission to distribute these, uh, mystery items to all the ladies."

Intrigued, I inquired, "What kind of mystery item are we talking about here?"

"You'll find out soon enough, Chloe. And believe me when I say it's definitely better when kept a surprise. Oh, that reminds me of the one rule you'll need to know."

This was getting more and more interesting by the minute.

"What's the rule?" I asked, playing along.

"You can't open this gift till you're alone with Dylan."

"Okay. I can wait."

"Trust me, you'll thank me afterward," she said, snickering.

I can't imagine what this gift could be.

"If only I had one clue," I murmur to myself when I arrive at the bar and grill and park.

When I get out, I see Aubrey is already here. She heads over to me, and sure enough, she does have a gift. It's hard to miss, what with neon green wrapping so bright it's glowing under the parking lot lights.

"Hmm, that sure is some megawatt-level gift wrap, Aubrey," I remark. "Is it a clue as to what's inside?"

I take the box, and she says, "Maybe, Chloe. You'll just have to wait and see."

"Aw, come on, you have to at least give me one clue. I'm dying here. And you know Dylan won't be home till day after tomorrow."

"I know," she says smugly. "But like I said—it'll be worth the wait."

I decide to go ahead and trust her on this one.

Placing the gift in the backseat of my car, I say, "I better leave it out here. I'd hate to accidentally leave my mystery gift in the restaurant."

Laughing, Aubrey says, "Jeez, no, that wouldn't be good. Someone else would have all the fun then."

*Hmm, it's something fun and I should only open it with Dylan...*

The clues start to come together and I get a feeling this gift is something sex-related, though I can't for the life of me figure out how the green paper relates.

"Shall we go in?" Aubrey asks.

"Absolutely, the game's starting soon."

After we're seated at a high-top table on the bar side of the restaurant, the game does indeed begin. We have a terrific view of the many TVs up on the walls, so when Brent scores early on, Aubrey and I are able to watch the entire play unfold.

"That was amazing," I say, in awe of Brent Oliver and his stellar offensive skills.

"That's my man," she states proudly.

The waiter comes over then, carrying two shots, which is odd since we didn't order any drinks or shots.

"These are from the guy at the end of the bar," he informs us, setting down the little glasses. "He said y'all seemed to be having so much fun that he wanted to buy you something to keep up the celebrating."

"Keep up the celebrating?" I look over at the bar.

But it's strange, as no one is seated where the waiter indicated.

"Who do you mean?" Aubrey asks. She's looking in the same direction. "There's no one sitting in that last bar stool."

"Huh, that's weird," the waiter says. "The guy was just there."

"Well, he's not there now," Aubrey replies.

"Do you even want these shots?" I ask her.

"Not really. This whole thing is kind of strange. Do you want them?"

"No."

We send the shots back and tell the waiter to let us know if the guy who bought them returns. I, in particular, would love to get a look at him. I have a sick feeling this may not be as random as it appears.

Aubrey, watching me closely, asks, "What's wrong, Chloe? You look really upset right now."

"I kind of am," I admit.

"Is it anything you want to talk about?"

"Actually, yes."

I need to share this with someone other than Dylan and my brother, so I tell her about the weird shit that's been going on—the slashed tire, the cigarette butts outside my bedroom window, and the weird scuffling noises.

Once I'm finished, she says, "Oh my God, that is both scary and bizarre."

"I know, right? I thought it was all over, but now I'm not so sure."

"Do you think the guy who sent us the shots was him?"

"Could've been," I say.

Sighing, she replies, "It's a shame he left. We could've nailed him."

"Yeah, it is too bad, but I'm sure he planned it like this."

"Do you have *any* idea who it could be?"

I shake my head no. "I originally thought it could be my ex, but Sten doesn't smoke…and he lives in Phoenix. That'd be one heck of a drive to make repeatedly just to harass someone."

Aubrey looks unsure. "I don't know, Chloe. The cigarette butts could've been to throw you off. And I hate to say it, but I've heard of cases where angry exes have traveled farther than that to do bad things. You really should think about hiring someone to look into exactly what your ex has been up to down in Phoenix."

"That's not a bad idea," I concede.

The rest of the evening is okay, but a pall has been cast over it. Even when the Wolves beat the Stars, I can't muster much enthusiasm. There are too many things on my mind.

Things like, what if Sten is my stalker?

And if it's not him, is it the guy who bought us shots, then disappeared?

Is *he* my stalker?

If so, that would mean my stalker knows everything I'm doing, every move I'm making.

And I'm all alone till Dylan gets back.

*Shit.*

# 21

# NO NEWS IS NOT NECESSARILY GOOD NEWS

## DYLAN

After the Dallas game, and once I'm back in my hotel room, I hear from the private investigator I hired.

He informs me that Sten is no longer in Phoenix. *Fuck.*

But he's also not in Las Vegas. *Hmmm…*

"What about somewhere else in the state of Nevada?" I query.

"There's no record of him there, either."

"That's good, yeah?"

"Maybe…"

Then it hits me.

"Shit. You just said there's no *record* of Sten being in Nevada. But that doesn't mean he's not there. He could be staying in motels and paying cash, or using an alias."

"Those are all possibilities," the investigator confirms.

*Christ.*

"This is so not good." I scrub my hand down my face. "That prick could be secretly holed up anywhere in the state, including Las Vegas."

"Yes," the PI says, and my heart sinks. "The fact remains that we have no idea where your girlfriend's ex-husband is at the moment. But don't worry, I'll find him."

That gives me no solace.

And I won't be home for two more days.

What I need is for Graham to stay with Chloe until I return.

I call him once I'm done with the PI and fill him in on what's been going on.

When I'm finished with all my updates, I say, "You know this Sten dude, Graham. Do *you* think it could be him? Could he be the one stalking Chloe?"

"It's a real possibility," Graham, to my dismay, replies.

"Shit," I groan.

"Don't worry. I'm heading over to her place right now. I don't care that it's almost midnight. Between the two of us, we can keep her covered twenty-four seven."

"Yeah, except when she's at the coffee shop. If we could just get Chloe to take some time off from work, I'd feel a lot better. That's the only place where we can't be with her."

"I'll talk to her," Graham says. "But if I know my sister, and I do, she can be really stubborn over certain things."

"No kidding."

Graham and I wrap up, and I feel relieved that Chloe won't be alone tonight or tomorrow.

But that feeling doesn't last long.

Chloe calls not five minutes later—my phone is blowing up

tonight—and informs me there's been a weird incident.

"What kind of weird incident?" I carefully inquire as I recall that her plans were to go out to eat with Aubrey. "Did something bad happen at dinner?"

"Kind of," she replies softly. "Or…I should say maybe. I'm not sure."

"Damn it."

I'm trying to hold it together for her sake, but truth is I want nothing more than to go right the fuck home now.

But I can't; I have another game tomorrow night in St. Louis.

All I can do is sit by helplessly, listening as Chloe tells me all about her "weird incident."

Some dude bought her and Aubrey shots. That wouldn't be concerning under normal circumstances—after all, they're two pretty girls that were out by themselves—but in this case, it wasn't a couple of guys hoping to talk to them. It was one guy, who left before they could see his face.

"I don't like this one bit," I state.

"I don't, either," Chloe replies.

Blowing out a breath, I ask, "Do you think it could be your ex? I know you said no, but something sure seems shady about this whole ordeal."

"I don't know if it's him," she replies, "maybe."

*Shit, before it was a definite no, but now it's a maybe.*

"This is so not good, Chloe."

"I know, Dylan. And I've been thinking… Do you think we should hire someone to find out what Sten's been up to lately?"

"Uh…"

"What is it?" she asks.

"I may have already taken a step in that direction."

"You hired a PI?"

"I did, and he's a good one. I hope you're not pissed that I did it without running it by you first."

"Are you kidding? I'm not mad at all. If anything, I'm disappointed in myself that I didn't take the initiative and do it when this all started. Anyway," she sighs. "Have you heard back from this investigator?"

"I did, actually. He called earlier."

Her tone is tentative as she asks, "What did he say?"

"He said that, for now, there's no evidence Sten is in Las Vegas."

I hear her sigh, surely in relief.

I hate that I'm about to ruin it for her when I add, "There's also no evidence that he's not there, Chloe. The problem is that he's definitely not in Phoenix."

"Crap."

"That was my reaction too."

"Dylan," Chloe begins, sounding chagrined, "I feel so bad for dragging you into my mess of a life."

"Hey, hey, don't say that. No one has dragged me anywhere. Good or bad, we're in this together."

Softly, she murmurs, "You're too good to be true, you sweet man."

"I'm whatever you need me to be, Chloe."

In the background, her doorbell rings. It has to be Graham. Shit, I forget to tell her I called him and asked if he could go over to her place tonight. She's going to think the worst.

And she does...

"Shit, Dylan, there's someone at my door. It's after midnight. This can't be good."

"No, wait, sweetheart, it's okay."

I go on to assuage her concern by sharing that I may have taken the liberty of enlisting her brother to stay with her the next two nights.

"That's probably him," I finish up with.

"Thank God," Chloe says on a sigh. "Let me go let the poor guy in."

"Check the peephole first," I remind her. "Just in case."

"I will."

I hear Graham's voice seconds later, along with Chloe's. He says to tell me "hello" and "not to worry."

Chloe returns to the call and we start to wrap up. "I'll talk to you tomorrow," she says.

"Okay."

"I love you, Dylan. And thank you for...just...everything."

"I love you too, sweetheart. I can't wait to get back to you."

"I know. I'm on countdown too."

Too bad the next thirty-six hours will, no doubt, be the longest of my life.

# 22

## GRAHAM TO THE RESCUE

### CHLOE

Graham is at my place and I already feel safer. But since it's late and we're both exhausted, I tell him I'm going to bed.

"Wait a second," he calls out, and I turn back around. "I wanted to talk to you about something before you run off."

"What?" I ask.

Sighing, Graham says, "You should've told me things had escalated, Chloe."

I go back over to the sofa and sit next to him.

"I thought I had it under control," I explain. "Nothing's happened lately. Well, until this thing at the bar and grill. But really, I haven't worried because Dylan's been here with me. The only visitor to my window lately has been a rabbit named Jack."

Leveling me with a *wtf* look, Graham says, "Do I even want to ask?"

"Uh…" I shake my head. "…probably not."

Dropping any further talk of Jack, he says, "Let's get back to this incident at the bar."

"Okay."

"So some mystery dude bought you and your friend shots, and then disappeared?"

"Yes."

"I don't like this at all, Chloe."

"I know, Graham, I don't either."

"Is it Sten?" he asks flatly.

I shrug. "I don't know. I didn't think so at first, seeing as he's supposed to be in Phoenix."

"But he's not."

"According to Dylan's PI, that's correct."

Graham jumps up and starts pacing. "Damn it, we need to know for sure where that crazy ex of yours is. This could all be him. And, really, when I think about it, who the hell else could it be?"

"Yeah," I concede, "I don't have any enemies that I know of."

Finally sitting back down, Graham says, "Well, it could be someone who got their eye on you. There are a whole lot of creeps out there in this world."

"Yes, unfortunately, there are." I sigh, feeling sad that his statement is so true. "I just don't know why some creep would target me."

Graham has some comforting words to say, but when I mention that I don't think I can sleep now, he says, "Why don't we watch something on TV? Who knows, maybe there's an old eighties movie on."

Nineties may be my go-to decade for music, but when it comes to classic movies, I'm a solid eighties girl.

Still, I'm hesitant. "I don't know, Graham. I don't think I can concentrate."

"You don't need to concentrate. But you'll feel better if you can get your mind on something else."

"Okay, I can try."

We turn on the TV, and Graham flips through the channels. We actually do find an old eighties movie, one we both love.

"*The Breakfast Club*," we yell out in tandem.

"Looks like it just started too," I add excitedly.

It's the perfect flick to take my mind off of things because it's one of my all-time favorites. Graham and I watch the movie, reciting lines we both know even before the actors say them.

We spend the next couple of hours laughing and having fun. I feel better, even though I know it won't last. Reality will come a-knocking, as it always does.

I only hope it doesn't shatter my life into a million pieces.

# 23

# A HUNDRED DIRTY THINGS WITH A SEX TOY

## DYLAN

The St. Louis game is looking to be a rout, and not in our favor. The Blues are clobbering us, and it's only the second period.

We're down 6-1 by the start of the third. And frankly, it's an embarrassment.

I get burned for the second time tonight in the final period when one of their star players takes off with my errant pass.

And just like that it's 7-1.

*Fuck.*

My head's just not in the game. How could it be? This crap with Chloe has me worried about far bigger things than hockey.

It feels as if a danger is closing in, and there's nothing I can do to stop it, especially not from this far away.

Frustrated, I suddenly high-stick an opponent. It's an accident, but

I, unfortunately, draw blood.

I'm called for a double minor, which means four minutes in the box. That's pretty much what's left of the game, so I won't see any more ice time. Not that it matters, since we're losing big-time.

After the game, I'm throwing shit around in my stall in the visiting team locker room like a mofo. It doesn't matter; all of us players are doing the same. Coach Townsend doesn't even bother yelling at us. He just shakes his head and leaves. His silence says more than him sticking around to lecture us ever would.

But our captain, Brent Oliver, has something to say.

"I think we all know we sucked big hairy balls tonight. No one out there played well."

"Hey, it's only one game," the always upbeat Benny Perry interjects.

"He has a point," I interject. "It is just one game. We should look at it as a one-off."

Brent thinks it over and says, "Okay, maybe. But it can't happen again. We're too close to playoff time. This one-off, or whatever, should be a wake-up call for us."

We all agree, and then Jaxon Holland, who's always up for a good time, chimes in with this gem: "Hey, I know what we should do tonight to put this shitty game behind us."

*Uh-oh.*

I glance over at him and notice right away that he has on his shit-eating grin.

"Do I even want to ask what you have in mind?" I say with a raised brow.

"You sure do, my man. There just happens to be a really famous strip club not far from our team ho—"

"Nope, I'm out."

Strip clubs have never been my scene, and they certainly aren't now that I have Chloe in my life. I'm content to simply head back to the hotel and hang out in my room. Our flight leaves ridiculously early tomorrow morning anyway.

When the shuttle finally drops us off at the team hotel, it's about midnight. I bid farewell to the guys abstaining from strip club antics and head up to my room.

After I'm settled, I take out my phone and call Chloe. It rings for a while, and I remember then that she has an early shift at the coffee shop in the morning.

I'm about to end the call, but then she picks up.

Since she sounds really sleepy, I ask her if I woke her up.

"No," she says, "I'm in bed, but I was reading."

"Is Graham still there?" I ask, immediately feeling fearful that she's alone.

"Yes. He's out in the living room watching TV."

Chuckling, I remark, "Man, your brother sure loves that flat screen he bought you."

"You're not kidding. I just about had to wrestle him for the remote so I could watch your game."

"What?" I pretend to be appalled. "He didn't already have it tuned in?"

"No, there was some football documentary on."

"Ah, that explains things. Well, I can't begrudge a man his chosen sport."

Chloe snickers. "You boys are too funny."

Lowering my voice, I rasp, "I'll show you funny, woman. You just wait till I get back tomorrow."

"I can't wait, Dylan."

"God, me too."

I'm set for some phone sex, but just then her brother yells in something from the other room.

"Your walls are way too thin," I remark when she returns her attention back to our call. "I heard everything he was saying."

"Yeah, he wanted to know where I keep—"

"Your secret stash of potato chips," I finish for her, since I heard it all anyway.

Laughing, she says, "Speaking of food, would you want to go out to eat tomorrow night?"

"Night? What's wrong with four or five in the afternoon?"

"Ugh, I kind of got talked into working a double tomorrow. I won't be done till nine."

Chloe is just too nice. I can't say anything bad about that, though. I'm glad she's not become a guarded or negative person. Even after everything she's been through, including the stalker shit, she remains positive.

"Later is fine," I say. "Do you want me to pick you up at the coffee shop after your double?"

"That's okay. I'm taking my car tomorrow. We can leave for dinner once I'm home. Or we could just order food in since it'll be kind of late."

"Babe, I'm fine with whatever you want to do."

I am too, but there is one thing weighing on me. Even though I'm happy Chloe will have her car, I don't like the idea of her walking out to the parking lot alone in the dark. Not with the stalker still out there.

Softly, she asks, "Why are you so quiet, Dylan?"

"I was just thinking… Can you have someone walk out with you tomorrow when you're done?"

"Yes, of course. I've been doing that lately anyway once it's dark out."

I breathe a sigh of relief. "Thank God."

We talk more, and soon we're joking and teasing.

"Oh, by the way," Chloe says at one point, "I totally forgot to mention that Aubrey gave me that gift she promised."

"What is it?" I ask.

"I don't know. I'm supposed to open it with you."

"Open it with me? Why?"

"It has to be sex-related, Dylan," she murmurs. "You know, like a toy."

"Hmm, with instructions to open it together, I'd say the probability of that is high."

"There is one weird part, though."

"Do tell."

"Aubrey claims the neon green paper she wrapped it in is a hint."

"A hint, huh?" I'm stumped too. "I have no idea how neon green wrapping paper relates to sex, sweetheart."

"Guess we'll find out soon enough."

"Guess we will."

After we're done talking, I lie back on the bed. I'm thoroughly intrigued as to what this sex-related gift from Aubrey could be. I could always ask Brent, but I'd rather it be a surprise for both me and Chloe.

Maybe when she returns from her shift tomorrow night, we can skip dinner and get straight to opening this mystery gift. If it's what we think it is, we can put it to good use.

"Hmm, this should be fun," I murmur as I reach down to my cock, thinking of a hundred dirty things I can do to Chloe with a sex toy.

# 24

## FULL-MOON CRAZY

### CHLOE

I head out to my car the next day to drive to the coffee shop for my double shift.

When I hop into the Fusion, I notice the green-wrapped gift from Aubrey is still lying in the backseat. I forgot about it initially, but even after I remembered I didn't think it'd be a good idea to bring it inside with my brother there. Graham would definitely expect me to open a gift. And no way am I opening a sex toy in front of my brother.

Talk about awkward!

But Graham is gone now. He left early this morning to go to his gym—a place I need to get back to soon—and then he's heading home to his own house afterward.

That means Dylan and I will have my place to ourselves tonight. *Yes!*

I feel upbeat and optimistic when I arrive at the coffee shop, but my light mood wanes as the day wears on. We're slammed with customers, and the two waitresses working are in the weeds in no time.

I help out by pulling double duty as barista *and* server. But it's frustrating because everyone seems pissed about something or other.

"I've been waiting here ten minutes and no one's come to my table. What kind of sucky place is this?"

"I asked for sugar-free syrup, miss, but there's sugar in this vanilla latte. I can tell, you know."

"Noooo, I wanted wheat bread for this sandwich, not white."

"This isn't toasted, miss. Please take it back."

At my wit's end, I slam that particular sandwich—for which I'm sure the woman stated "not toasted" when she ordered—onto a counter in the back, out of view of the customers. Hell, they're mad enough as it is. No need for them to witness my mini-meltdown.

"Whoa, Chloe," says one of the waitresses, Dee, as she lets out a low whistle. "Who pissed in your Wheaties this morning?"

"Ha ha. It's not me, Dee, it's everyone else. They're *all* mad today, it seems."

"They are exceptionally ornery," she agrees.

I then muse, "You know what? I bet there's going to be a full moon tonight."

"Hmm, we'll see," she says.

Sure enough, a few hours later when Dee and I are in the back room again, taking a breather from the madness, she moves the curtain aside on the small window facing the side of the building and says, "Hey, you were right earlier. There is a big ole full moon out there. Damn."

Triumphant, I declare, "I knew it."

The full-moon craziness continues, but nothing can prepare me for when two uniformed police officers step into the shop and ask for the owner of the white Ford Fusion parked out back.

"Um…" I raise my hand sheepishly. "That would be me."

It's near nine, the end of my double shift and closing time for the store. Thankfully there are no more customers to contend with, so I'm able to take off my apron and come out from behind the counter to talk with the officers with no audience looking on.

Save for Dee, who mouths, "Let me know if you need me," before she scurries off to the back.

"What's going on?" I ask the policemen.

One is an old grizzled veteran-type, and the other is a young rookie.

The grizzled one says, "So the Fusion is yours, miss?"

"Yes, it is. Is there a problem with my car?"

The young one, sighing heavily, says, "I think you should step outside with us so we can show you what's at issue here."

"Show me what's at issue?" A sick feeling comes over me. "What the heck is going on?"

"Just follow us, please."

They start out the door, and I trail along behind them. But I still have no clue what's happening. Even when we reach the back lot where the employees park, I can't see past them to my car.

But then I step to the side and—

"Oh my God, who would do such a thing?"

The bright glow of the full moon and the small streetlamp nearby cast an eerie pall over my severely vandalized car. Both taillights are busted out, and someone has sprayed red paint all over the doors, the trunk, and the hood. But the worst part is what has been written.

Things like, "Die Bitch Die" and "Sluts Burn in Hell."

*What the fuck?*

"W-who would do this?" I stammer as I walk around my car, only to come upon more nasty slurs.

"That's what we were hoping you could shed some light on," the older officer says.

"I have no idea who could be so sick, but there's a camera—" I point to the back of the coffee shop, to where a camera *should* be. "Wait, it's gone. What the hell is going on?"

The officers make a note to ask the owner if the camera was taken down for repair, or if whoever vandalized my car removed it. It wasn't placed all that high and could easily be reached if someone climbed up on one of the dumpsters.

I start shaking and I just can't stop.

"I-I don't know who did this."

I get that much out before I'm choked up by a sob.

And then I say, "If I knew, I'd tell you."

"Miss, miss, it's all right." That's the older guy trying to sound soothing, but looking really uncomfortable. "We'll find out who did this."

"How will you do that?" I cry out. "The camera's gone."

"There may be witnesses," the rookie chimes in. "Someone called this in anonymously. They saw the car when they came around back to throw away their empty bags in the dumpster. Anyway, we can trace that call and see if that person saw more."

"They could've seen the perp taking off," the older officer adds encouragingly.

That doesn't make me feel much better, and I utter a soft, "I'm scared."

"That's to be expected," the rookie says. "But rest assured, we'll catch whoever did this."

This has to be the work of my stalker, and I know I have to tell them.

Quietly, I state, "There's been more than just this one incident."

The officers both turn to me.

"How do you mean?" the veteran asks.

Sighing, I fill them in on everything. Afterward, they decide to have my car impounded. Before the tow truck arrives, I'm sure to discreetly slip the "gift" from Aubrey into my purse.

*Phew, close call!* Can't have the police confiscating a toy I never got to try out.

But things grow serious again when the rookie says, "Your vehicle will be towed to a secure facility where we can dust for prints."

That just scares me even more. It's like these officers are getting their ducks in a row for if something really big happens.

But what could be bigger than this?

I can think of only one thing—the stalker physically harms me.

# 25

# ESCALATION

## DYLAN

I receive a frantic call from Chloe, who is running really late from her long shift at the coffee shop.

"Wait, slow down," I urge when her words are obscured by sobbing.

She doesn't, but when I do catch "police" and "vandalized," I am out the door.

"I'm coming now," I tell her.

Chloe is still on the phone with me as I jump into my car so we talk the whole way there. I've never been happier that I own a Ferrari as I make it to the coffee shop in record time.

The cop standing next to Chloe glares at me as I screech into the back lot, but neither he nor his younger partner say a word when I jump out and race over to Chloe, both of us lowering our phones at the same time.

The officers no doubt see I'm a man on a mission, a mission to comfort the woman I love.

My arms encircle her slight form, reminding me of just how vulnerable she is.

"Oh, Dylan," she cries.

"Shh, shh," I say comfortingly. "It's going to be just fine. We'll find the bastard who did this."

"But who could it be?" She steps back, wiping away her tears. "Who could hate me this freaking much?"

Despite what my PI had to say, my money's on Sten. I mention this to the officers and they take down the info, along with more from Chloe.

"In situations like these," the older officer says, "the ex is often the perpetrator."

Chloe's face drains of color, and I know then that for her, the thought of Sten doing this is far worse than if it were a stranger. He must really scare the shit out of her. Maybe that's why she's been in a sort of denial that it could be him. I think she's been hoping to God that it's not.

My blood boils thinking that her prick ex could have her so terrified.

"If it's Sten, Chloe, I swear…"

I'm careful not to blurt out anything that'll land me in hot water with the police, but the officers are no dummies.

The older one, eyeing me up, warns, "Sir, it is imperative that you let the police handle this."

"I will." I sigh. "I'm just venting."

I think the younger officer has recognized that I'm a Wolves player.

He hasn't said much, and he's been watching me with the kind of awe fans often do.

Sure enough, before we go our separate ways, he quietly pulls me aside and says, "Hey, I know now's not the time, but I wanted to say good luck with the rest of the season."

"Thanks," I murmur.

Chloe and I then walk over to the Ferrari, where I say to her, "We need to catch the motherfucker who's after you. This has gone too far."

"I know," she replies, running both hands through her golden hair. "It's weird, though. Things have been so quiet at home. The camera hasn't captured anything other than Jack eating the carrots I put out for him."

"Whoever this is must've noticed the camera and decided harassing you at work would be the next move."

"This is an escalation, Dylan. So what the hell comes next?"

That's something neither of us cares to consider.

# 26

## UH-OH

### CHLOE

'm not really all that hungry after the incident at the coffee shop, so I ask Dylan if we can skip dinner.

"Whatever you want to do is fine with me," he replies.

But then I'm reconsidering when, as we're driving back to my place, my stomach emits an angry growl.

Dylan, glancing over, says, "You sure you don't want to stop and pick up some food? You actually should try to eat something, Chloe."

"Mmm, I don't know," I murmur. "I feel a little nauseated."

"What's the last thing you had to eat?"

I think about it…and think about it…

"Chloe?" he prompts.

"I'm not really sure," I admit at last. "I had a bagel with some cream cheese. I think that was around noon."

"That's it." Dylan makes the next right, into an area filled with stores and restaurants. "We're getting you some kind of sustenance, babe."

I dispense with any argument since my stomach rumbles again as the aromas from the many restaurants assault my nose.

"Ooh." I point to one of my favorite places. "What about Chinese?"

Chuckling, Dylan says, "Sounds good to me."

A short while later we're seated on my living room floor, sharing kung pao chicken and szechuan shrimp. Seems I was hungrier than I even realized.

"Oh my goodness, this food is the best," I say around a mouthful.

Dylan laughs and agrees, "It is pretty good."

Laughing or not, he still looks worried. So I bring up what we've not yet talked about.

"You think Sten vandalized my car, don't you? You think this has all been him since the start?"

Dylan sets down his chopsticks. "I think he's the most likely culprit, yes."

I can't deny that it makes the most sense, but…

"There's one thing that has me stumped."

"What's that?"

"The cigarette butts outside my window." I gesture in the direction of my bedroom and said window. "Sten doesn't smoke."

"Maybe he didn't smoke while he was with you. Or maybe he just kept it from you. Who knows? He sounds a little crazy, so he could've even just lit cigarettes and stubbed them out. You know, to purposely throw you off."

"I did consider that," I admit.

"Chloe, he makes the most sense as the perpetrator. This is clearly someone with a lot of pent-up rage against, uh…"

"Me," I finish for him. "It's okay to say it. It's the truth. And it does make the most sense that this would be Sten. Does your PI know where he is yet?"

"Not yet. But he's really good. He'll find out soon enough."

I'm comforted by the fact that the police and Dylan's private investigator are out there looking for answers. I just hope we get some before it's too late.

A few days later, I hear from one of the officers in charge of my case. He has some news. It's the older veteran I'm speaking with, and though in my state of upset I missed it the other night, I now learn that his name is Officer Willet.

"What kind of news do you have?" I ask, hopeful that he'll say the perpetrator has been caught and this nightmare is over.

No such luck.

Instead, he says, "We were able to lift some unknown prints from your car."

Since I went down to the station yesterday to be fingerprinted in order to rule out my own prints, I get excited.

"Ooh, do you know who did it then?"

"I'm afraid not, Miss Tettersaw. The prints came back from our database as unidentifiable."

"What does that even mean?" I ask.

"It means that the person responsible has never been processed. He or she is not in the system."

I don't know whether this is a good or bad thing. Maybe since it's not someone in the system, they're new to criminal life and not a major threat. Or, and this is the bad possibility, they could be so smart that they've never gotten caught.

That one makes me ill.

I let out a little choking sound, and Officer Willet asks, "Are you all right, miss?"

"Yes, yes, I just had a tickle in my throat," I fib.

"Okay, well, we'll be in touch with when you can pick up your car."

"Thanks," I murmur.

After the call, I sit on the sofa for a long time, trying to recall if Sten ever mentioned having trouble with the law…for anything…ever.

Problem is that it never came up. I just assumed he hadn't done anything criminal in his past.

Now I wish I'd outright asked.

Because I now can't rule him out.

*Crap.*

# 27

# EAT YOUR HEART OUT AREA 51

## DYLAN

This upcoming Saturday night there's a charity event with the Wolves. It's a big fancy ball where everyone will be dressed to the nines. I want Chloe to come with me. Not only is she my one and only, but a distraction from the stalker will be good for her.

"Be my date," I say after telling her all about the event.

It's late in the morning, and I've just returned from practice. We're talking in her bedroom since sleepyhead doesn't have to work today and has been lounging around in her pajamas reading romance novels.

"Oh, I don't know, Dylan." She sets her Kindle down on the bed and sits cross-legged. "So much has been going on lately."

"I know, sweetheart, but this is a perfect opportunity to forget about the craziness of late."

From the look on her face, I realize I've said something wrong.

Chloe's nerves are frayed so it's to be expected.

Throwing her hands up in the air, she exasperatedly states, "Forget? How can I forget about any of this? My life is pure crazy these days."

"Babe…" I sit on the edge of the bed and place my hand on her knee. "I don't mean that you should forget about what's going on. I just mean you should get out and have some fun for one night."

Chagrined, she says, "I'm sorry, Dylan. You're absolutely right. I know you're only trying to help." She scoots over and leans her head against my shoulder. "I'm not mad at you."

I put my arm around her. "I know, sweetheart."

"It's just that this stress is really getting to me."

I reach up and cradle her head. "I understand and it's fine."

Softly, she murmurs, "I clearly *do* need a night out."

"Are you saying you want to go then?"

"Yes."

"Then it's decided."

The pressure is on. I absolutely must make the charity ball an amazing night for Chloe.

Good thing I have a brilliant plan on just how to accomplish that.

The ball is held at a swanky resort outside of the city. It's as elegant and formal as I expected it to be. The ballroom is opulent and could pass for a palace interior.

Good thing all of us players and our dates are dressed like royalty.

I'm wearing a black tux and tails, and Chloe is my real-life princess. She's a vision of beauty in a powder-blue sparkly sequin ball gown and matching glittery red-soled heels. Her long blonde hair, purple tips a perfect accent, is up in an elaborate twist.

"You look exquisite tonight," I relay to her as we step out onto the ballroom floor for our first dance.

"Hmm…" She smiles mischievously as her arms slide up around my neck. "You don't look so bad yourself, Mr. Hot Hockey Player."

When she scans down my body and bites her lip, I have to chuckle. "Uh-oh, I know that look."

No coy Chloe tonight as she outright declares, "That's right, Dylan. You just wait till I get you home later."

We begin to dance then, though I'm ready to take her home right the hell now so she can make good on that promise.

*Ah, but the time will come.*

Chloe is having a good time here at the ball, and that's all that matters. It's good to see her in such a carefree mood. She definitely needed this.

"Are you happy?" I ask as I pull her closer to me.

"I am," she murmurs, leaning her head against my chest. "I really am."

I love her so much. But I feel like where we are currently is just not enough. I want us to be more than this. Hell, we're already practically living together, why not make it official.

Leaning back slightly, I say, "I'd like to ask you something, Chloe. And it's kind of important."

She tilts her head to the side. "Okay?"

"How do you feel about moving in with me?"

Looking confused, she says, "Do you mean not just temporarily?"

"No. I mean for good."

She slows to a stop, even though the music is still playing.

Peering up at me with an indecipherable expression, she murmurs an equally indecipherable, "I, uh…um…"

*Uh-oh, this can't be good.*

*She thinks it's too soon.*

*Or maybe she fears I'm proposing a change to our current living situation because I'd rather stay at my own house.*

*Shit, is she worried that I'm only asking because she has a stalker?*

I voice all these concerns to her, in that exact order, and then I state, "I'm asking you to move in with me because I love you, Chloe. I want to be around you as much as possible because I feel like what we have together is something really special. It feels right to take the next step. I just hope you think so too."

"Dylan, I…" Tears well in her eyes. "I do feel the same way. But I don't know what to say."

"Say yes." I chuckle nervously. "But only if you want to."

"I want to." She begins smiling, and then she starts laughing. "So yes, my answer is yes. I'll move in with you."

"Are you sure?" I double-check.

"I'm surer about this than I've been about anything lately. I'm just overwhelmed is all. But in a good way."

"Ah, well that's a relief to hear."

She peers down at my tux, and then at her own fancy attire. "I feel like a princess. And you certainly look like a prince."

"So this is a fairy tale?"

"Yes." She chuckles. "But it's *our* fairy tale."

I tighten my arms around her. "Yes, darling, it is."

A couple almost bumps into us then, and we realize we're still not moving.

"Uh-oh, people are starting to stare at us," I murmur as I glance around.

"I see that," Chloe whispers.

"Uh, I think we better start dancing, princess."

"Ah, yes. I think so too, my prince."

We start dancing again and after a minute or two of swaying to and fro, I whisper in Chloe's ear, "For the record, I think I just might be the happiest man in this room tonight."

"I'm really happy too," she replies. And then she adds mischievously, "Oh, and by the way, what I said earlier about you just waiting till I get you home tonight, it still holds true, now more than ever."

"Shit, I hate that we have to wait."

"Oh, but we do."

She's right; it'll be awhile before the charity event ends. But that's okay. I'm with the woman I love.

And what do we do?

We dance more, drink champagne, and eat a fabulous dinner of lobster and steak with our friends.

Brent and Aubrey are seated at our table, as are Nolan and Lainey, and Benny and Eliza. I talk a lot of hockey talk with the boys, but at one point I do overhear the women giggling and going on and on about... Area 51?

*Huh?*

I've never known Chloe to be into aliens and the paranormal, but who knows?

Later in the evening, after the event is over and when Chloe and I are on our way to my house, I bring up the topic.

"Chloe," I begin, clearing my throat. "I heard you talking with the girls at dinner and I just have to ask you how in the hell did Area 51 come up?"

"Oh, that." She lets out a soft chuckle. "It wasn't exactly a conversation about the real Area 51."

Hmm, she's smiling that wicked grin again.

So I ask, "Is it something sex-related, by chance?"

"It just may be, Dylan. It just may be."

"You're killing me here, babe."

Leaning over, she places her hand on my thigh. "Okay, I'll tell you what's up."

"Uh, it's going to be me that's 'up' if you move that hand any higher."

"Dylan!"

She then begins… "So Aubrey's sister, Lainey, happened to let it slip what our neon green-wrapped gift is. And let's just say that it's Area 51–themed and definitely something we can use in the bedroom."

Interest piqued, I ask, "So it's a sex toy for sure?"

"Yes."

"An Area 51–themed sex toy?"

"It would seem so."

"Fuck."

"Yes, fuck indeed." Chloe laughs. "There's about to be a lot of that going on."

"Hell, woman, you're not kidding."

At my house, Chloe and I can't reach the bedroom fast enough. And once we're there, the real fun begins.

I make short work of her ball gown, leaving it in a sparkling mess puddle on the floor. The moonlight streaming in illuminates the gown, but it's Chloe I'm watching as she lies down on my bed.

"You really are my princess," I murmur as I crawl atop her. "You're my beautiful, smart, and strong princess."

Her fingers weave into my hair. "I am, and this princess wants you, Dylan."

I wind my hand down between us to find she's wet and ready for me.

"Don't make me wait," she moans as I part her folds.

"I'm not going to," I assure her as I replace my hand with my cock, gliding along her silky softness.

"Your pussy feels so good, sweetheart," I murmur. "You're always so ready for me."

"That's why you should slip inside me, Dylan." She arches her hips, an invitation that I respond to by plunging into her.

"Yesss," she hisses.

"Do you like that?"

"Uh-huh."

I pull out and thrust back into her roughly.

"I don't think I heard you," I tease. "Tell me how much you like it hard."

"I do, I do," she pants.

She wiggles her hips, taunting me, tempting me, but I make her wait.

"I haven't heard the words, Chloe."

"I like it hard and fast," she practically yells.

I love that I can undo her like this.

"Now fuck me, damn it."

Well, shit, how am I supposed to hold back from that?

I don't—I plunge into Chloe with renewed fervor, fucking her until we come together.

Afterward, we doze off, but only for a short while. When we awake, we snuggle some more and whisper sweet nothings to each other.

When her hot little body presses up to mine invitingly, I'm ready for round two.

Arching a brow, I ask, "Do you want to open that gift from Aubrey?"

Hooking her leg over my hip and feeling how hard I am, she murmurs, "Yes, I think we should."

I go retrieve the gift from the dresser. That's where I've been keeping it after Chloe gave it to me to hold onto after her car was towed.

"Finally, we're opening it," I say.

Chloe sits up and agrees, "Right. I can't wait to see what it looks like."

"Yeah, me too."

Green neon wrapping goes flying, and suddenly I'm holding up a big fake dick in the streaming moonlight.

"Wow, it really is Area 51–themed."

The bright green color gives it away, but the 51 printed on the side of the fake shaft leaves no doubt.

Chloe's watching my every move with great interest. Or maybe it's the fluorescent lime-green dick that has her fascinated. It is quite a sight.

"Bring it over," she purrs. "And do it fast."

Whoa, someone wants to play.

Good, I do too.

My erection was waning, but I'm back at full mast as I imagine the many ways I can "probe" Chloe with this alien cock.

Back in bed, I accidentally turn on a switch and the toy begins wiggling in my hand.

"That looks, um, interesting," Chloe remarks.

Arching a brow, I say, "I'm betting this is gonna feel pretty good, Chlo."

"Let's see!"

She sure is anxious to give this thing a go.

So we do.

And then things get even *more* interesting.

As I'm working Area 51's magic on her, the thing begins to glow. It seems the more excited she becomes, the brighter it gets. Pretty soon the whole room is bathed in green.

It's otherworldly, that's for sure. I suspect even more so for Chloe, as she's panting and moaning, and then shuddering with what looks to be an intense orgasm.

"Damn, Dylan," she gasps afterward as she's catching her breath. "That was amazing."

"Like out-of-this-world amazing?" I inquire with a smirk.

"Something like that."

I'm propped up on my elbows over her and she urges me down, down, down.

"I think though, Dylan," she goes on. "I'm ready for you to bring me back down to Earth."

Eat your heart out Area 51. This is something only I can do.

# 28

## WHERE'S JACK?

### CHLOE

I start packing in preparation for my move to Dylan's house. I can't wait to live with him at his place. It's been fun having him stay with me off and on, but he actually owns his house. Plus, like he mentioned, it's far roomier than mine.

The timing couldn't be more perfect too. The next step, number nine, in the X Your Ex pamphlet is "Throw Away Something from the Past."

Well, as of this moment, I'm throwing away something I brought back with me from Phoenix, something intangible—my fear.

I never thought I'd reach this point, but look how far I've come.

There will be no more second-guessing when something feels right, like how it feels for me and Dylan. I love that man with every fiber of my being, and I'm no longer afraid to show him that in every way.

If I get hurt in the process, so be it. At least I'll know I gave it my all, and the fear of rejection or hurt didn't hold me back.

"I am ready to get started on this new life," I proclaim as I finish packing.

I head to the kitchen for a glass of water, and as I'm peering out the window to a view I won't see much longer, I realize something.

"Oh my God, I can't leave Jack!"

How will my rabbit friend make it without me? He's used to a steady food supply. Not to mention, he's practically tame. What if he trusts the wrong person and it ends badly?

I shudder at the thought.

Plus, there's this—Dylan may be convinced Jack is feral, but I am not. I still think he's a domestic rabbit. I mean, he sticks close to the back of my place most of the time, never wandering off too far. And lately when I go outside to feed him—not just carrots but now rabbit food as well—he hops right up to me.

Coupled with all the other reasons, I declare, "That's it. I'm taking him with me."

Resolved that this is the right thing to do, I fill his little metal bowl with food pellets and take it out to him.

"Jack. Jack!" I call out.

*Huh, no response. So much for him coming right up to me and not wandering off.*

"Guess he's busy doing rabbit things," I mumble dejectedly as I set his food down in the usual spot.

I head back inside to scour for a box big enough to fit a rabbit in comfortably. I'm pretty happy when I find a roomy one. *This will do.* I make a lining of super-soft towels and a teeny, tiny pillow and I'm ready to go check if he's shown up yet.

First, though, I should probably call Dylan to make sure he's okay with this. I don't care to show up with a furry roommate that's unwanted.

I make the call, and after I inform him I'm done packing, I say, "So I have a question."

Dylan says, "Go ahead, shoot."

"How would you feel about me bringing along a buddy?"

With a smile in his tone, he inquires, "What kind of buddy are we talking about here? An Area 51 kind of friend?"

That, though a misunderstanding, makes me laugh. "Ha, of course *he's* coming."

"Just like you'll be next time we put him to use," he rasps.

I sigh contentedly. Dylan's lusty voice always works me up, but sadly there's no time for this. I need to get back to asking how he feels about adopting Jack.

Clearing my throat, I say, "Okay, enough, mind out of the gutter for both of us. When I said I wanted to bring along a buddy, I meant something furry."

"That's not helping get my mind out of the gutter, Chloe," he deadpans.

"Oh my God, Dylan, stop."

He agrees, albeit reluctantly, to behave.

Finally, I get to the point of the call. "If it's okay with you, I'd like to bring along Jack."

"The rabbit?"

"Yes. And before you start up on how he's a wild animal, I'm telling you that he's not. I'm almost certain the people who lived next door left him behind. So we can't just abandon him. He's used to us, and he's accustomed to being fed. I don't even want to think what might happen to the little guy if—"

"Chloe, Chloe. I'm fine with Jack. Bring him along. I'm sure he'll love the back of my house. There's way more room to roam around, and everything is fenced in, so it's safer. If he's a domestic rabbit, like you think he is, I'll even build him a hutch."

That was easy. Dylan really is the polar opposite of Sten.

Still, I feel the need to double-check. "You're really okay with this?"

"Absolutely, babe. I like the little guy too."

My love for Dylan soars to new heights. I mean, a man who loves bunnies? How cute is that?

"Did I ever tell you how much I love you?" I gush.

"You may have mentioned something about it this morning, but I think you better refresh my memory."

I mull it over and come up with the best comparison, something that's sure to resonate with him. "I love you even more than *you* love hockey."

"Wow, that's really saying a lot, babe."

"I know, right?"

"Well, I love you too."

"More than you love hockey?" I'm throwing it out there, but with a fun note in my voice so he knows he needn't choose.

"Uh, let's not go there," he replies.

"Dylan!"

*I was just kidding. He better choose, damn it!*

"Okay, okay. How about if I say I love you in a different way than I love hockey?"

"I think I can accept that." And then I add, "Look, I know we're talking apples and oranges here."

"If that's the case," he responds, his tone light, "then you're the apple of my eye."

"Pfft, you're so corny."

"But you love me anyway, right?"

"I do."

After a few more sappy proclamations of love, we hang up and I resume my search for Jack.

But still, there's no sign of him anywhere out back.

"Where in the heck are you, little guy?" I say on a sigh.

I check once more a short while later. This time I cover the ground all around my place, as well as the area around the empty unit. But again—there's no Jack.

"Maybe he moved," I murmur. "Nah, that seems unlikely."

He could be out getting some, right? I mean, he is a rabbit and they multiply like crazy.

Well, I'm not giving up. I plan to check back every day once I'm gone. I'll need to put out food for him anyway.

I try to reassure myself that everything's okay, but the truth is there's something about Jack being missing that's not sitting well with me…at all.

# 29

# A NEW MEANING TO BLESS THIS HOUSE

## DYLAN

There's a game tonight. And since there was one last night as well, there's no practice in the morning.

That means I have time on my hands till this evening.

"So why not move Chloe into my house today?" I ask myself.

I see no reason not to, so I call her to see how she feels about moving up moving day.

Only problem is it's seven in the morning so, of course, I wake up sleepyhead.

Yawning, she listens to my proposal, murmuring a tired, "Mmm," as I finish.

Since that's not an answer, I ask, "So what do you think?"

"That works for me, Dylan. Let's do it."

"Okay, great, when should I come over?"

Starting to sound more awake, she says, "Now is fine. I'll jump in the shower and get dressed as soon as we get off the phone."

Hearing the words "get off" and the thought of Chloe in the shower leads me to ask, "Shit, you want to wait for me?"

Laughing, she replies, "No way. You know we'll never get me moved if we start *that* up."

I sigh. "Yeah, you have a point. Expect me in about an hour then. I'll stop and rent us a moving truck on my way over."

"I think a van will be fine. I don't have all that much."

"A van it is," I say.

The rental place where I secure the van isn't all that busy. I have time to spare to stop at a local pet store and buy a pet carrier for Jack. Chloe told me she made up a box for him, but this is more secure. Plus, I think this'll show her I really am fine with the bunny coming to live at my place.

"It looks like the right size," I say to Chloe once I arrive at her doorstep.

"Hmm, let me take a look." She takes the carrier from me and holds it aloft, examining it from multiple angles.

Man, she must really love that rabbit. I sure hope he shows up soon or she's going to be crushed.

"I think he'll fit in here comfortably," she declares at last. "It's better than the cardboard box I was planning to use. That is, use if we ever see Jack again."

Chloe is clearly feeling down, so I pull her in for a hug.

"He'll show up," I assure her. "He's bound to get hungry sooner or later."

"I hope it's sooner rather than later," she murmurs against my chest.

*Shit, I hope so too.*

We finally begin loading her boxes into the moving van. As we do, I sync my phone to her Beats Pill so we can jam to eighties and nineties music as we work.

We end up having to make a couple of trips from her house to mine, but all in all, we finish up relatively early.

"Hey," I remark as we're standing in my living room, "I think I can still get in a power nap before I need to drive down to the stadium for the game."

Chloe knows that's my usual game-day routine and replies, "That's good, Dylan."

I raise a brow. "You want to join me?"

I've been staring at her luscious ass all day in her hot-as-fuck shorts, and I am so ready to get them off of her.

Playing it coy, she demurely asks, "What exactly are you suggesting?"

"Oh, I think you know. Besides, now that you're an official occupant we need to properly christen this house."

"Hmm, I think we've taken care of that, like, multiple times," she reminds me. "It's not like I've never been here before."

I wrap my arms around her. "Yes, but you were never actually *living* here. Now you are."

I lay her back on the sofa, and hovering over her, I rasp, "This is your house now too, so let's make it official. We'll start in here."

Her shorts are off in no time, and I'm pounding into her just as quickly.

"Fuck, this is so good."

"Yes, Dylan, yes," she groans.

I feel her shuddering beneath me, coming apart, but I'm not ready for this to end.

I have a lot more in the tank, so to speak, so I suggest, "Do you want to move this to the kitchen?"

She looks up at me, sex-flushed and disheveled. "The kitchen?"

"Yes." I hoist her up, and she wraps her legs around me. "There are a lot more rooms to christen, Chloe my love, so we may as well check that one off next."

She laughs, but not for long. Once she's bent over the kitchen counter, pert little ass in the air, I have her gasping and moaning in no time.

"Fuck me, Dylan. Yes, just like that," she demands.

I drive into her.

And then I have her over my shoulder caveman-style, where I'm off to deposit her on the dining room floor. She crawls on top of me and rides me till she comes all over my cock.

Then we're off to the study, where we do it on the desk.

"I can't hold off much longer," I warn her.

"So don't," she says. "We can check off more rooms later."

*Ah, thank God.*

I pump and pump, till I'm filling her with my love.

Afterward, I lie down on the desk surface next to her.

"Good thing you have a big desk," she murmurs.

"Among other big things…"

Laughing, she says, "Cocky much?"

"More like confident."

"Well," she concedes, "you do have every right. Not only is your dick big, but you sure know what to do with it."

I hold her closer. "Aw, thanks, babe."

"Mmm," she sighs contentedly. "I hope we stay like this, wanting to have sex all over the house all the time."

"Well, we'll be like this for a while. We have a lot more rooms to go."

"And when we've christened them all?"

"Maybe I'll put on an addition."

That makes her laugh. And laughing makes her breasts jiggle, which makes me hard once more.

"Have you ever done it against a washer when the spin cycle's on?" I ask.

"I can't say that I have, Dylan."

"Oh, shit, you're missing out, sweetheart."

But not for long.

The laundry room is checked off next.

# A COMING STORM

## CHLOE

hate that Dylan has to leave for his game. If I had my way, we wouldn't leave the house till we hit *all* the rooms.

We finally do make it up to the bedroom, but only to rest. Dylan has to get in his before-game power nap, after all. Plus, I could use a few post-multi-orgasm *z*'s of my own.

So sleep it is.

When I wake up a short while later, Dylan is already up and about. He's quietly padding around the room, gloriously naked.

"Are you sure you don't want to come watch us kick some Jets ass tonight?" he asks when he notices I'm awake.

I sit up so I can better enjoy the naked-Dylan show, but then he finds a pair of sweatpants and pulls them on, thus putting an end to my ogling.

Ooh, maybe not, though.

The sweatpants hang low on his waist, so his muscular chest, ripped abs, and the insanely sexy V of his tapered waist are still on full display.

"Chloe, did you hear me?"

"Huh?"

When I scan up to his face, I find his brow is raised.

*Oops, busted.*

Chuckling, he asks, "Did you hear *any* of what I just said?"

"Was it something about the game tonight?" I venture.

"Yes. I was wondering if you'd like to go."

I think it over. I would like to go, but there's so much still to do here. With a sad sigh, I decline.

"I'll just go to your next home game. I really need to stay and unpack."

"Okay, sweetheart, I understand."

Suddenly, our attention is diverted when thunder rumbles off in the distance.

"Well, that's something you don't hear every day in the desert," I remark.

"That's for sure."

Dylan pads over to the window and, peering out at the darkening sky, he says, "I'm kind of glad now that you are staying in tonight. There's definitely a storm brewing."

Another crash in the distance has me jumping out of my skin. "Yikes, it sounds like it's going to be a bad one."

One thing about rain in the desert is that it's an all-or-nothing kind of thing. There'll be no precipitation for ages, but when the rains do come, and they always do, they are often torrential. Flash flooding is not uncommon.

And that's exactly what happens.

A few hours later, after Dylan is long gone and I'm unpacking my fourth box of clothes, a weathercaster on TV reports that several side roads are flooded, and electricity is out in some places.

"Be careful, folks," he warns. "If you don't need to go out tonight, stay home."

I'm not too worried about Dylan. He'll be returning home via the freeway, which is, as of this last report, not flooded.

But I am concerned for someone—Jack.

*What if the area around my old place is flooded?*

*What if Jack's in trouble?*

*Who's going to help the poor little guy?*

"No one, that's who," I murmur as I'm plagued by those awful thoughts.

Crap. I can't take it anymore. I decide to take my chances and go check on him.

First, though, I send a text to Dylan informing him of my intentions. He won't receive it till the game is over, but at least he'll be aware of where I am and what I'm doing.

I then realize I'll need to borrow one of his cars. My Fusion is out of police custody, but it's now at the body shop being repainted.

Sighing, I grab the keys for Dylan's Range Rover and send him another text so he doesn't think it's been stolen when he gets home and finds it's gone.

*It'd be super embarrassing to get arrested my first day of living at your house,* I type with a chuckle.

With that done, I proceed to run around procuring what I think I'll need to conduct a bunny search out in the rain. The carrier Dylan so thoughtfully purchased is a definite must. An umbrella is in order too, though it takes me forever and a day to find one of those. I finally locate a big one in a closet, but even more time is wasted when I have to rummage through boxes and boxes of unpacked clothes in search of my seldom-used raincoat.

"There it is!" I cry out when I find the olive green jacket.

Finally, I'm ready to hit the road.

I check my phone for progress on the game and find that it just ended. I consider waiting for Dylan, but it'll be a while before he gets home.

"I can totally do this on my own," I remind myself, enforcing my new assertion that fear no longer rules my life.

And with that, I'm off.

The rain has let up considerably, so the drive is pretty fast.

I'm feeling like this won't take long at all—till I see the whole complex is engulfed in darkness.

*Great, there's no electricity. This would have to be a spot where it's out.*

"Just my luck," I murmur.

Determined nonetheless, I pull into my old parking spot and hop out of the car. I decide to leave the umbrella behind since the rain is nothing more than a fine mist at the moment. But I do retrieve the carrier from the backseat and take my phone out of my purse so I can stuff it into a jacket pocket.

When I toss my purse back in, the pepper spray from Dylan rolls out. Since it's creepy and desolate, you bet your ass I grab that thing.

*Look at me, taking my safety into my own hands. Dylan would be proud.*

There's nothing left to do but go find Jack.

Only problem is it's really, really dark behind my old unit. And that makes it scary as hell.

Taking a breath, I whip out my phone and activate the flashlight app. And then I forge onward.

I am a woman on a mission, armed with illumination and pepper spray, damn it. What could possibly go wrong?

Just as I'm thinking those go-me thoughts, I trip over a rock and almost face-plant into the sandy, though now mushy with rainwater, earth.

"Shit, crap."

Just as I'm righting myself, a prickly cactus stabs my leg.

"Ouch, damn it!" I drop the carrier. "Did that thing move on its own?"

It didn't of course, but things are getting really creepy. Escalating the fear factor, I suddenly detect one of those damn scuffling noises from up ahead.

Shining the light out in front of me, I call out, "W-w-who's there?"

My heart, already beating like a damn jackhammer, starts to pound out of my chest. Even so, I make sure my pepper spray is ready so I can defend myself. If some bad person is back here with me they're about to get more than they bargained for.

But then fear, or maybe common sense, kicks in—I need to abort this mission, a fact driven home when I hear the weird scuffling noise again. It's one thing to be fearless; it's another to be stupid.

But before I can hightail it out, something small and furry and sopping wet hops out from behind a shrub.

"Jack!" I exclaim, exhaling a relieved breath. "It's just you, thank God."

I rush toward him just as the rain starts back up. *Great.*

And then, out of nowhere, I am pushed hard from behind.

"What the…?"

I fall forward onto my knees and Jack takes off.

I somehow remain calm enough to take a quick inventory…

I have my phone and my pepper spray. And you know what? I have every intention of fighting back.

Scrambling to my feet, I spin around to face whoever just shoved me.

Shining my light out in front of me, pepper spray in hand, I grind out, "Bring it on, motherfucker."

Someone laughs.

I adjust the light and—*fuuuck*. "Sten?"

"So you haven't forgotten about me, after all," he snarks.

My ire rises because it's all so clear now. There's no more denial, so I go ahead and call him out.

"You're the one who's been stalking me. It's been you all along, hasn't it, you slimy prick?"

"Watch your language, bitch."

I laugh bitterly. "You can't shut me up anymore. I can say whatever I—"

And that's when he rushes me.

"Fuck you!" I scream as I raise my pepper spray, ready to blast him in the face.

He's quicker, though, and knocks the canister out of my hand, along with my phone.

Unarmed now in any way, I do the only thing left to do—I freaking run.

# 31

# SHE DID *WHAT*?

## DYLAN

We're kicking the Jets's asses, just like I knew we would.

And personally I am having an outstanding game.

First period, I assist on a beautiful goal by Benny Perry.

Second period finds me blocking shots and battling in the corners like a mofo.

By the third period, the Wolves are up 5-1.

And then it's suddenly 6-1 when I initiate a breakout from the defensive zone and shoot the puck into the net.

After our decisive victory, I grant a couple of on-ice interviews, and then it's off to the locker room to get ready to go home.

"Good game, man," Noel, my defense partner, says to me as he's taking off his equipment at the stall next to mine.

"Yeah, you too," I reply.

There are more congratulations, along with an "attaboy" talk to the team from Coach Townsend.

And, dude, when all is said and done I feel like a million bucks. Not only is our team firing on all cylinders as of late, but I finally feel at peace in so many ways.

The past was catching up to me, but no longer. Sure, I still live with regrets that I couldn't save my mother—I'm sure I always will—but I've learned not to beat myself up about it anymore.

Watching Chloe change from a victim to a strong person inspires me every day to be better, do better. I was a victim too back then, as I was just a kid. I finally accept that now.

I guess you could say love saved me.

Flying high, well, on everything, I hit the showers. Afterward, I have a chance to chill and check my phone. I expect to find a text or two from Chloe, probably a progress report on how unpacking is coming along.

What I don't anticipate, seeing as it's a stormy and dangerous night, is a message from Chloe that she's out looking for that damn rabbit.

"Is she crazy?" I mutter.

Jaxon Holland is packing up his bag next to me and says, "Who are you talking about?"

"Chloe," I murmur.

He throws his bag over his shoulder, readying to leave. "Is she okay?"

"I'm not sure, man." Grabbing up my own bag, I say, "Hey, I'll walk out with you."

"Cool," he replies.

As we head out to our cars, where the rain is pouring, we put up our umbrellas and I prepare to fill him in on what's going on.

"Are you ready for this?" I begin. "Chloe's out in this fucking weather looking for a rabbit that used to hang out in her backyard."

"You mean she's over at that place she just moved out of?" he asks.

"That would be the one."

"Shit, it's a bad night out," he says, the wind whipping around us like a mini tornado. "Not to mention, it's dark as fuck and no one's really out. Is there even security over there?"

"No."

My apprehension is rising, and it just about goes through the roof when Jaxon shakes his head and says, "That's bad, Culderway. I hear electricity is out all over the city."

"Aw, fuck, you've got to be kidding me. I better get over there right now."

Jaxon offers to come with me, as we've reached our cars, but I decline.

"Thanks, man, but I got this."

We go our separate ways and once I'm out of the rain, I text Chloe a quick message to hold tight—*the game's over and I'm on my way, babe.*

Funny that she doesn't text anything back.

# 32

## FIGHTING BACK

### CHLOE

Running is the best option.

But I don't get too far.

Sten catches up to me in what feels like an instant, grabbing me in a tight hold from behind.

Struggling to break free, I shout, "Get the hell off of me!"

"You fucking whore," he hisses in my ear. "You moved in with him, didn't you?"

I play dumb, hoping to keep the jerk from flipping out.

"I don't know who you mean," I murmur.

"Yes, you do," he snarls. "I'm talking about that hockey guy."

Angry, though still struggling, I pant out, "What I do is none of your business anymore."

He, tightening his arms around me till I'm immobile, whispers forebodingly, "You'll always be my business, Chloe."

Shit, this is him showing me he had control from the start. Allowing me to struggle was designed to wear me out, which it unfortunately has.

Breathing hard, I go limp.

The rain has slowed to a light mist again, which is unfortunate. Sten's hold is not slippery in the least; it's freaking rock solid. The only thing I can do to slow him from doing whatever he has planned is to keep him talking.

So I once again ask, "Are you my stalker? Is that why you're here in Vegas—to stalk me, harass me, vandalize my car?"

"That car should be in my name, Chloe. I bought it."

I have my answer. *Shit.*

Defeated, I mumble, "It is you, isn't it? You're my stalker."

"Yes," he replies as he sniffs my hair. *Eww!* "I've been following you, watching you, because I still want you. I did those things to get your attention. Did it work? Do you still want me too?"

*Uh-oh, it's time to tread carefully. He's talking crazy now.*

The answer is, of course, no. But I can't just blab that out. Sten is clearly unstable.

"Chloe?" he prompts.

"Um…"

He starts kissing my neck. *Ugh.*

"I even started smoking," he murmurs, chuckling sinisterly. "You drove me to it, my love."

*My love?* This is worse than him calling me nasty names. It's like he's delusional on top of everything else. I really need to get away from him…and fast.

But how?

My pepper spray is gone, so that's out. So what are my other options?

I can think of only one—I must rely on my self-defense training.

My sapped strength is slowly returning and with it, a clearer train of thought. The moves my brother taught me for when your assailant has you in a hold from behind are coming back to me.

And I'm ready to use them.

Bending my knees quickly, I shoot my hands up in the air as fast as I can.

It works! Sten's hold on me is broken, and I spin around quickly so he can't grab me again.

"What the fuck?" he bites out.

He sure didn't expect that.

*And he's not going to expect this*, I think as I knee him in the groin as hard as I can.

That freaking drops him.

But I know he won't be down for long. I need to get out of here.

Blindly, I take off into the darkness.

As I round the corner of the other side of the unit, I slam straight into a hard body, a definitely male hard body.

*Shit, does Sten have an accomplice?*

Adrenaline still pumping, I'm blinded by rage.

*Damn it, I'll take this bastard on too.*

Weak and mousy Chloe is gone for good.

Yelling and screaming and kicking and clawing, I fight this person with everything I have.

But the asshole seems unfazed and still somehow grabs hold of me.

I thrash and battle, one last stand.

But then I hear a voice that calms me. *Huh?*

"Chloe, Chloe, it's me, Dylan. Calm down, sweetheart."

*Oh my God, it's Dylan.*

*I'm safe, I'm safe!*

Relieved, I collapse into my savior's arms.

# 33

# THIS ONE'S FROM ME, ASSHOLE

## DYLAN

I turn Chloe around to face me, and I keep on repeating, "I'm here. I'm here. You're okay. Everything is all right."

I'm not sure why she was fighting me, but something sure terrified her. For her to not even see me, to instantly snap. "Sweetheart, what happened?" I ask.

"Dylan" is all she can choke out since she's fighting back tears.

I rub her back. "It's okay. Everything is fine now, Chloe."

"No, no, it's not," she cries, gesturing to a big lump on the ground several feet away.

It's the first I've noticed it, whatever "it" is. "What the fuck is that?"

"Not what, Dylan, but who."

My eyes still aren't fully adjusted to the darkness, but I suddenly remember I grabbed a flashlight from the car before I got out. In all the confusion, I forgot to turn it on.

I do so now and shine it up ahead.

"Stay where you are!" I yell out when I see the lump is a man, currently trying to stand.

The guy rises to his knees, but otherwise obeys.

Through clenched teeth, I ask Chloe, "Did that fucker hurt you?"

*If she says yes, this guy's a dead man. Okay, maybe not dead, but he'll be severely incapacitated.*

"He tried," she says, "but I fought him off and kicked him in the balls."

"Whoa, that's my girl."

Sighing, she murmurs, "That guy is Sten, Dylan. It was him all along stalking me. You were right. And so were the police."

"Wait." I point over to the guy, who I notice is kind of holding his junk. "*That* is your fucking ex?"

"Yes. He's the one who's been doing all the awful things, like vandalizing my car. It was all him from the start."

"Well, it ends here, Chloe. It ends now."

Whipping out my phone, I call 911.

By the time I'm done talking with the call, Sten is standing. *That impudent little fucker.* He doesn't appear to be a flight risk, though. He looks like he's still in pain, what with the way he's holding his crotch.

"You clearly got in one hell of a shot," I say to my ass-kicking girlfriend.

"I did," she confirms, looking proud as can be.

She has every right to be pleased with herself. She's come a long way. Subduing this bastard on her own has to have been cathartic for her.

But, you know what? I need a little catharsis too.

I tell Chloe to stay put, and then I stride on over to Sten.

"What do you want?" he snarls. "I heard you call the police. I'm not gonna run."

"You better not," I warn him.

"Guess you and the little whore can be happy now," he taunts.

Asshat never sees it coming when I cock back my fist and nail him in the jaw.

"Aw, fuck."

He teeters and drops back to the ground.

"Stay down there," I spit. "You belong in the mud."

The prick deserves so much more, but I'll let the police deal with him.

"You're not worth it," I say.

When I return to Chloe, she's shaking. The adrenaline rush from this whole ordeal is wearing off.

"I'm cold, Dylan," she says.

"Here, sweetheart, take this."

I take off my jacket and wrap it around her.

The police arrive a few minutes later. They hear our stories and arrest Sten. Officer Willet is on the scene and informs us that he'll be in touch.

After everyone is gone, save for Chloe and myself, we gather up the pet carrier and locate her pepper spray under a shrub.

"Too bad Sten's not still here," she says, holding up the spray. "I could blast him once for good measure."

"Don't worry," I assure her, "you got him pretty good with that knee to his balls."

Chloe doesn't respond to that. She just leans into me, clearly exhausted.

"Where to now?" I ask softly.

"I just want to go straight home, to *our* house."

"You got it, babe."

# 34

# JACK!

## CHLOE

Sten is charged with a slew of offenses. Since he can't make bail, he's left to rot in a jail cell till a court date is set.

*Now that's justice.*

I'm proud of how I handled myself, and Dylan is too. I want to continue taking responsibility for my own safety, so more self-defense classes are definitely in order. What Graham taught me has already proved invaluable.

So, a couple of mornings after the incident with Sten, and while Dylan's at practice, I call my brother to see if he's up for meeting at his gym.

"I'm already there," he tells me with a laugh.

"Perfect. I'll be right over."

"Cool. See you soon."

I arrive at the gym ready to roll.

"Let's get started," I say to Graham as I'm grabbing up a pair of sparring gloves.

He loves that I'm so pumped, but since I haven't mentioned what went down the other night with Sten, he's naturally confused.

"What's brought on this renewed interest in learning to fight, Chloe? You haven't been to the gym for a while."

We're stepping into the boxing ring, and I'm already bouncing on my toes, taking pretend shots at my brother. "Nothing, dude," I reply. "I'm just excited to get back at it."

Graham crosses his arms over his massive chest and stares at me. "Don't bullshit me, Chloe. Something triggered this."

I quit juking and jiving, knowing it's time to come clean.

"Okay, okay. There is something I need to tell you."

I proceed to fill him in on everything that happened, sparing no detail.

"And you're just telling me this now!" he exclaims once I'm finished. "You should've called me right away. In fact, you should've called me before the police arrived. I would've liked to have had a few minutes alone with that worthless ex of yours."

"I'm sure you would have, Graham, but that would've ended with you in trouble too."

"Yeah, you're probably right."

Pulling me in for a brotherly hug, he says softly, "I'm just happy you're okay. That fucking Sten was the stalker, huh? I had a feeling. Thank Christ he's off the streets. He can't harm you ever again."

I sigh and take a step back, not as confident on that last.

"He couldn't make bail, so we're good for now. Let's just hope the judge throws the book at him."

Graham assures me, "I'm here for you, Chloe. I'll testify if you need me to."

"I know that, Graham. And I really appreciate how you're *always* here for me. You're the best brother ever."

He really is the best brother. And he's an amazing teacher. I tell him as much, and I let him know that the moves he taught me helped me subdue Sten.

"They really do work," I marvel.

"They sure do," he agrees. "But there's a lot more you can learn."

I start bouncing again like a prizefighter, fists up.

"Well then, I guess we better get started."

When I return from the gym, wow, am I ever sore! Graham did not go easy on me. But that's good. I want to feel empowered, like I really did work out and learn something.

Dylan is still at practice, so I head upstairs to take a long, hot bath.

My phone buzzes on the way, and since I don't recognize the number, I answer with a tentative, "Hello?"

A gruff voice inquires, "Is this Chloe Tettersaw?"

"Yes."

"This is Officer Willet, ma'am."

*Ma'am?* He makes me feel so old. Maybe it's just police protocol, like a formality. But then again, maybe it means something more serious is afoot.

Suddenly worried that the charges against Sten are about to be dropped, or something equally awful, I ask, "Is everything okay?"

"All is fine," he replies. "I'm not calling for any bad reason. I just have a question."

"Oh, thank God," I breathe out, relieved.

Clearing his throat, he says, "So I was back at your old apartment this morning, checking on some details for my report, and I came across a rather friendly creature."

"A rabbit?" I question, hopeful.

"Yes."

"That's Jack!" I exclaim, thrilled and happy. "I was wondering what happened to him. He ran off the other night when all that bad stuff went down."

"Ah, so he is yours," Officer Willet murmurs. "I figured that was the case. You'll be happy to hear then that I apprehended him for you."

"Apprehended him?"

Laughing, he says, "Sorry, hazards of the job. What I meant to say is I caught your rabbit and brought him back to the station."

"You caught Jack? You must be like the rabbit whisperer. He usually only comes up to me, and sometimes Dylan."

"I don't know about that rabbit whisperer part." He laughs. "But maybe you're onto something since catching him was really easy. I just picked up a carrot that was lying on the ground and held it out to the little guy. He hopped right on over."

"Wow, I guess feeding him really has made him tame."

Officer Willet sounds perplexed. "Made him tame?"

"Yes."

*But wait, maybe I've been right all along and Jack is a domesticated rabbit.* Here's my chance for a second opinion, and from a rabbit whisperer to boot.

"Officer Willet, my boyfriend thinks Jack is a wild animal, a jackrabbit to be exact. That's why I was saying we tamed him."

He starts laughing and laughing. Once he calms, he says, "That rabbit isn't wild by any means, and it doesn't take a rabbit whisperer to know that. Your Jack is not a jackrabbit. He's a domestic rabbit, Miss Tettersaw."

"I knew it," I state, feeling victorious. *Wait till I gloat to Dylan.*

"I always suspected he was abandoned," I go on, "but Dylan kept insisting he was wild. I'd almost begun to believe it."

"No, no, he was someone's pet at one time."

"Well, I'd really like to give him a home, if that's okay."

"Of course, Miss Tettersaw, I'd expect nothing less."

We make arrangements for me to pick up Jack, and I'm so excited that once I'm off the phone I immediately text Dylan with the good news.

*Jack is back!* I write. *And Officer Willet has him.*

*Great,* he texts back. *Is it okay for us to keep him then? I mean, even though he's a wild animal.*

And the gloating begins…

*He's not a wild animal. He's a domestic bunny. I was right all along.*

*He is, huh? Guess I better stick to hockey.*

*Aw, worry. You're still an expert on LOTS of other things, Dylan.*

*You bet I am. And I'm thinking maybe I need to demonstrate one particular area of expertise as soon as I get home.*

Hell, I can't pick up Jack and get back to the house fast enough.

# 35

# LIKE RABBITS

## DYLAN

Chloe and I decide that though the Wolves mascot is a wolf—no surprise there—our own personal mascot should be a rabbit. For one very specific reason—we go at it like bunnies all the time.

"It's perfect," I declare, after "going at it" in round two of today's sex-a-thon. "A rabbit as our mascot totally fits."

"For sure," Chloe purrs as she's lying next to me on the bed.

Slowly rolling over onto me, she starts rubbing our bodies together. "Mmm, maybe we should do it again. You know, to celebrate a rabbit being our mascot."

"I couldn't agree more," I murmur as I trail my hand down to cup where she's hot and always ready for me. "Fuck, Chloe. I can't wait to get back inside you."

"So do it now, Dylan."

She lines up our bodies so I only need to thrust up into her.

Will I ever get sick of this woman? No chance in hell.

Reveling in how lucky I am that she's mine, I possess her with my cock. I can't get inside of her deep enough, though, so I flip her over onto her back and slam into her with abandon.

"Don't stop," she pants.

"Never," I rasp.

When Chloe shatters around me, she brings me along with her. Afterward, I collapse onto her, and she holds me, rubbing my back. "I love you," she whispers.

"I more than love you," I reply, lifting my head so I can gaze into her gorgeous blues. "I worship you. You're my life, my love, my Chloe."

"Aw, Dylan"—she cups the side of my face—"you're so sweet to me."

"Always, my love, always."

It's true. I'm always going to love her. I know we're in it for the long haul, and so does she. I will marry this woman, that's a given. And I hope someday we have children, because if there's one thing I want in this world, it's to be a father. My own dad passed away when I was so young. And the jerk who came after, my horrid stepdad, was a monster.

I just want my chance to be the best father I can be—or at least give it one hell of a shot.

"What are you thinking about?" Chloe asks.

I roll onto my back and rest my arm behind me on a pillow. "Just thinking about our future, is all."

Teasingly, she asks, "Do you see it being long and bright?"

"Long, for sure." I chuckle as I peer over at her. "And as for bright, I think as long as we have Area 51 in our lives, that's a given."

She swats my arm. "Dylan, you're so bad."

"Oh, but you love it, though."

"I do."

Clearing her throat, she blows out a breath and announces, "What I'd also love is some food. How long have we been up here in the bedroom, anyway?"

"A long time." I laugh.

"Well, I'm starving." Chloe gets out of bed to slip on a robe. "And Jack's probably hungry too."

She's so caring and nurturing to that rabbit. I just know she's going to make a great mom someday.

Man, the future is really on my mind. And frankly, I can't wait for it to get started.

# 36

## JACK HAS A SURPRISE

### CHLOE

Soon I am completely settled into my new home. And I find myself in full nesting mode.

But I'm not the only one feeling that way—it seems Jack's in nesting mode too.

It's adorable, actually. Dylan has built him a cute little hutch out back, and Jack freaking loves it.

Our rabbit also apparently *loves* to eat.

"I don't recall him chowing down on this much at my old place," I remark one afternoon when Dylan and I are out back with our sweet little pet.

I don't mention that I've also been eating more than my fair share lately. I guess feeling happy and contented makes a person hungrier than usual.

And with that, I take a big bite out of the chocolate candy bar I've been working on. But before Dylan notices and starts teasing me about my increased appetite, I quickly stuff the evidence back into the big pocket on the front of my hoodie.

I don't know why I bother being sly, though. Dylan is preoccupied with adding more straw to Jack's hutch and not even looking at me.

"Yeah, he is eating a lot more," he murmurs distractedly.

Walking over to the hutch, I ask, "Hey, what's up? Why do you keep staring into Jack's new home?"

Pointing to back in the inside corner, he says, "Check this out."

I have to step over Jack to see into the hutch, as he's munching away on grass and makes no move to get out of my way.

*Silly bunny.*

As I peer into the hutch, I say to Dylan, "I'm not sure what I'm looking for. It just looks like a typical rabbit home."

"No, no, in the very back, Chloe, look there. Jack's made a nest with all the straw I've been putting in every day."

"Hmm, there sure is a lot of it," I murmur as I peer in.

And then I see what Dylan is referring to—behind all the new straw he just added is a comfy-looking mound of straw and grass that has a distinct indented center.

"Aw, it does look like a nest," I muse, glancing down at Jack, who is still eating. "Wait, do you think Jack looks different in any way?"

"How do you mean?" Dylan asks.

"Is he chubbier than he was, say, even a few days ago?"

Dylan rubs at the scruff on his chin. "Hmm, now that you mention, I think his belly is definitely bigger."

"Oh, crap, Dylan."

"What?"

Softly, like the rabbit might hear and somehow understand me, I murmur, "Do you think Jack could be *pregnant*?"

Dylan starts laughing. "Need I remind you that Jack is a boy?"

"Unless…"

Our eyes meet, and his widen. "Whoa, you think Jack could be a girl?"

"I do. There's a good possibility we've been wrong all along. Our Jack could very well be a Jackie. We never checked, you know?"

"Do we even know how?"

I look down at our rabbit. "Um, maybe we could lift up his little tail and have a peek?"

"Okay, I'll do it. But what am I looking for?" Dylan asks as he crouches down.

"I guess balls."

"Are they big on a bunny?"

"Guess we'll find out."

But we find out nothing. It's like Jack knows what we're up to, and after eyeing up Dylan suspiciously, he hops away.

"Catch him," I say.

"I'm trying."

Seems our rabbit, chubby or not, is evasive when he needs to be.

"He has better moves than our top line forwards," Dylan remarks as he makes an unsuccessful grab for Jack.

The slippery bunny takes cover under a clump of decorative grasses, and I throw my hands up in the air.

"Oh, hell, just give it up for now. He's too upset."

"That went well," Dylan deadpans as he stands and straightens his rumpled T-shirt and cargo shorts.

I roll my eyes. "Maybe we should let a professional handle this."

"Like a vet?" he asks.

"No," I laugh. "I meant me."

He waves his hand in the direction of the grass clump Jack is under and says, "Go for it, babe. Good luck."

I try to lure Jack out with carrots, but he's not falling for it. He hops away. But he has to cross a stone path to get to the next hiding place, a thorny shrub.

"Got you now," I declare when I try to cut him off at the pass.

Ah, but he's a wily rabbit. He hops to the left, jumps to the right. I try to keep up with him, but land on my ass. "Ouch."

I haven't fallen like this since my ice-skating lesson, and as Dylan helps me up, I rub my sore bottom.

"That hurt worse than falling on the ice," I mutter.

"Poor Chloe, I can always kiss it and make it better."

"Mmm, maybe later," I purr.

We ultimately give up on catching Jack to see if he has balls or not. I just end up making an appointment to take him to the vet the next morning.

I do check on Dylan's balls later, but that's a whole other story. It involves licking and sucking, and reminding him that he made a promise to kiss my sore ass and make it feel better. He doesn't spend much time on my butt cheeks, but he does a lot of kissing in a nearby area.

Yeah, we just can't get enough of each other. *Sigh.*

The next day, the vet appointment looms. But Dylan can't go with me because he has practice.

I load Jack into the pet carrier on my own, and then I'm off.

I'm informed rather quickly at the vet's office that our rabbit is definitely a girl.

And then there's more—she is indeed pregnant!

"Oh my God, are you sure?" I ask the vet.

He prints out an ultrasound image—yes, they can do that for bunnies—and hands it to me.

"Look there," he says.

"It's hard to make out," I remark as I turn the image this way and that. "But it looks like there are four in there. Is that right?"

"That's correct," the vet confirms. "Four little bunnies are on their way."

"Wow."

Jack is officially christened Jackie before I leave the vet's office.

I ask her if she likes her new name as I place her carrier into the car, but she just wiggles her nose at me.

"I'm going to take that as a yes," I state.

There is one thing bothering me, though. How in the hell did Jackie get pregnant? I never noticed any other rabbits around my old apartment. In fact, I never even saw any others in the entire neighborhood.

Ah, but then I remember—my girl was once in police custody.

"That has to be where you were defiled," I murmur as I fasten my seatbelt.

Jackie makes a little sneezing noise, like a dissent, and I peer over at her and say, "Hmm, sounds like you wanted it just as much. Guess bunnies need love too."

On my way home, I call Officer Willet to get to the bottom of the paternity mystery. He'll know if Jackie was ever in the presence of other rabbits while in lockup.

After I'm paged through, I get to the point of my call right away. "Was my rabbit in solitary confinement at the station?"

Officer Willet laughs. I think he likes me using police lingo like he does.

"No," he replies, "yours was in a room with another rabbit that day."

Somewhat incredulous—really, what are the chances—I ask, "Are there really that many convict rabbits on the loose?"

Chuckling, he says, "Usually, no. We're generally not even in the animal control business, but that day was unusual. An officer happened to find a rabbit at a crime scene and removed it till it could be retrieved by a humane officer. Since we're short on space here at the station, we didn't see any harm in placing the two rabbits together. If I recall, they seemed to like each other quite a bit."

"That would be a severe understatement," I murmur.

"Miss Tettersaw, has something come up with your rabbit? A problem of some sort?"

"I should say so," I exclaim. "That convict crime scene bunny you put in with mine knocked her up."

"Wait, I thought your rabbit was a male?"

"Clearly, *she* is not."

Trying, not very successfully, to stifle a chuckle, he says, "I am so sorry, Miss Tettersaw. We really had no idea."

"I should sue the city for bunny support!"

"Hell, don't do that."

"I'm just kidding," I assure him.

"Actually," he begins, sounding like he just thought of something, "this may work out."

"In what way?"

"Well, my daughter just turned twelve, and she's been bugging me and the wife for a pet of some sort. A rabbit would work out better than a dog or cat, so if it's okay with you I'd like to adopt one of the babies once they're weaned."

I'm thrilled to have a home for one bunny already, especially with the rabbit whisperer.

"Wow, thanks, Officer Willet. That'd be amazing."

On that happy note, we wrap up our call and I'm left feeling pretty positive about things. Maybe Jackie's impending motherhood isn't such a bad thing, after all.

"One down, three to go," I say to her as I park.

She wiggles her nose at me, and I add, "Don't worry, we'll find good homes for all your furry kids."

Once I have Jackie around back, I let her out of the pet carrier. She's so cute, hopping around, eating all of Dylan's ornamental grasses.

*Heehee, I'm so bad.*

I did my homework first and made sure none of the plants in the back are harmful to her. That's why I now give her the go-ahead.

"Go to town, girl. You're eating for *five*."

I realize then that I'm a little hungry as well, so I head inside to make a sandwich.

A few minutes later, as I'm taking the first gooey bite of a sure-to-be delicious grilled cheese, I start thinking about Jackie and her condition.

"I suppose I'll have to have her spayed after this is all over," I muse. "It's not like she can go get a Depo shot like me."

Speaking of which...when *was* my last Depo shot?

With everything going on, I've completely lost track.

I do some quick calculations in my head and realize my last injection was—*shit!*—in October.

It's now the end of March.

*Gulp.*

# 37

## MORE THAN WORDS

### DYLAN

Practice is running a little later than usual since Coach has us putting in more ice time. We're pretty much a lock for the playoffs, so he says it's essential.

When I do finally arrive home, the house is quiet.

*That's weird. Where's Chloe?*

"Sweetheart," I call out, concerned since she should be back from the vet's office by now. "Are you home?"

From the kitchen, she softly replies, "I'm in here, Dylan."

Relieved, I head that way, only to find her seated at the kitchen table biting her nails.

Uh-oh, this isn't like her at all. Something's not right.

"Chloe…" I rush over and pull up a chair. "What's wrong?"

My head is everywhere.

*Does she regret moving in with me?*

*Does she no longer love me?*

*Fuck, does she think this was all a massive mistake?*

Since we're committed to always being honest and upfront, I man up and ask her if any of those things are true.

"Of course not," she answers.

*So why's she swiping away a tear?*

"Why are you crying?" I ask. "You're obviously sad about something."

"No, no," she insists. "I'm actually happy. Truly, these are tears of *joy*, Dylan."

"Are they really, Chloe?"

Sighing, she says, "Yes. I swear I love living here. And I love *you* more than words."

That fills me with relief. But why are there still tears in her eyes? I need to think of something to whisk them away.

I think back to our beginning, to one of our best nights.

"'More than words,'" eh," I begin with a smile. "I know that one. It's one of your nineties one-hit wonders, isn't it? The title of an Extreme song, I believe."

She looks at me all confused, but hey, there are no more tears.

So I go on…

"Wait, I got it. You're crying because this is the start of another epic eighties-versus-nineties music battle and you *know* you're going down."

"Dylan," she says, laughing now. "You're impossible."

I need to keep her smiling, this is good, and the music references seem to be working.

So I say, "Hmm, 'Impossible', huh? Let me think. That's a Shontelle song, but it's too recent, babe, so I'm going to have to disqualify you."

This is all silliness, but who cares? Chloe is full-on laughing now.

Pushing a strand of blonde hair from her face and tucking it behind her ear, I say, "In all seriousness, though, why were you crying? It looked like there was more behind those tears. You looked… I don't know, sweetheart, confused, maybe?"

She glances away. "Uh, you know I took the rabbit to the vet today, right?"

Ah, she's deflecting, but that's okay. We'll get to the bottom of this.

For now, I just say, "Yes, I was going to ask you about that."

"Well, we finally have an answer to our burning balls question."

"Ouch." I wince. "Do you have to phrase it like that?"

That gets me another laugh, and then she informs me that Jack is no longer Jack. "She is officially named Jackie," Chloe states.

"Ah, so she is a girl."

"Yes, and there's more."

"What?"

"She's also definitely preggers."

"Wow, I wonder who the baby daddy is."

Huffing, she informs me, "Oh, I have an answer to that. The baby daddy is some crime scene rabbit that was down at the police station with our baby girl."

"You're kidding."

"Nope, Officer Willet filled me in on the whole sordid tale."

Chloe brings me up to speed on the rabbit loving that went down, and I conclude, "Guess our girl likes bad boys."

"It would seem so. We're definitely going to have to keep an eye on what kind of rogue rabbits she associates with from this point on."

Chloe comes over then to sit in my lap. She wraps me up in a hug and murmurs, "Maybe she'll find herself a nice hockey player rabbit down the road."

Leaning back, and with our foreheads touching, I whisper, "Like you did?"

"Yes, like I did."

"Chloe, seriously, what else is going on? I know there's more."

Sitting up straight, though still in my lap, she informs me, "There is, but I'm kind of scared to say what's weighing on me."

"Why? You know you can tell me anything."

"I know. But this is huge…and unexpected."

"Uh-oh, now I'm worried. What is it?"

She takes a deep breath, and then says, "Dylan, I'm pregnant."

"What?" I almost pass out.

But then the impact of what Chloe has just told me begins to sink in. And you know what? I'm okay with it. In fact, I'm better than okay with it.

I share this with her, and she says, "Are you sure you're not mad?"

"Are you kidding? I feel blessed."

"Oh, Dylan, thank God, because I do too. Those tears you saw earlier really were tears of joy. But still, I was worried about how you'd feel."

"Well, I'm happy," I assure her as I kiss her nose, her cheeks, and her lips.

We linger for a minute, and then I lean back. "Chloe, I have something to tell you too. And like your news, it's all good."

"So what is it, Dylan?"

"I want to tell you how I feel about you, like deep inside. You're my new beginning, sweetheart. You have been since the day we met. And as we got to know each other you became my salvation. You quieted all the internal demons I was battling. *You* put them to rest. So it really is time to turn the page and look to the future. I once thought I was saving you, but it's you who saved me. It's always been you, Chloe, and I suspect it always will be."

"That's beautiful, Dylan, and I appreciate it so much. But maybe we saved each other." Chloe's hands are in my hair, her lips on my neck. "So the only question left is what do we do now?"

"Oh, babe, that's an easy one. We have a baby."

# EPILOGUE

## EMBRACE THE UNEXPECTED

### CHLOE

*Several months later...*

In the move from my old place to Dylan's house, I somehow misplaced my X Your Ex booklet. I searched for months and months, going through box after box, but to no avail.

And then, one November day, it turns up.

I race into the kitchen where Dylan is eating his post-practice lunch and announce, "Hey, check out what I just found."

He looks up from where he's biting into an apple. "Wow, where was that thing?"

I sit down at the table with him. "I found it stuck under the flap of one of my old moving boxes."

"Huh, no wonder it took so long to show up."

"No worries, I have it now."

"Yes, you do."

I hold the booklet up. "You know what this means, right?"

"You can give it back to Graham?"

I roll my eyes. "No, silly man, it means that I can *finally* complete the tenth and final step in the program."

Chuckling, Dylan says, "Sweetheart, that's wonderful, but I really think you 'exed your ex' a long time ago."

"Hmm, you do have a point."

He's right. I've moved on. And as for Sten, he's about as exed out as any ex could ever get. He remains in prison, not just for what he did to me but for many other things. It turns out that ole Sten was committing a slew of white-collar crimes that no one knew of. Well, until it all came to light before his first court date. He pled guilty in the hopes of receiving a lighter sentence, but the judge gave him the longest sentence possible.

Let's just say that man won't be out on the streets anytime soon.

But I don't dwell on the past, and I certainly don't lose any sleep over Sten. I look only to the future these days—and the present, of course.

Still, I want to finish the program. I'm just weird like that. My brother would say it's a Tettersaw trait, but I think it's just me.

In any case, I say to Dylan, "If you remember, I did the first nine steps and they really changed my life. I should at least check out what the tenth one is."

"Go for it," he says.

Finished with his lunch, he stands and comes over to linger behind me so he can look over my shoulder. That man is just as curious as I am to see what the final step is.

"Dun-dun-dun," I murmur as I flip to the back.

"And there it is," I proclaim as I turn the page to step ten.

Dylan looks down, reading along with me. And then we both start to laugh.

"Wow. You completed step ten a long time ago, babe, and you didn't even know it."

"Yes, I did," I murmur, feeling a wave of satisfaction.

Step ten is "Embrace the Unexpected," which is something I did several months ago—as did Dylan—when we found out about Autumn. By the way, Autumn is our perfect little six-week-old baby girl.

Shortly after we found out I was pregnant, Dylan and I got married. It was a small ceremony, but perfect nonetheless. Many of his teammates attended, and Aubrey was my maid of honor. Graham, of course, was Dylan's best man.

Fall then arrived, and so did our girl. Our beautiful daughter was a few weeks early, but she's doing great now.

Speaking of which, she lets out a little squeal from where she's sleeping in the next room. Or I should say, *was* sleeping.

"Someone just woke up," Dylan remarks.

I go to her and bring her to us.

"She's just amazing, isn't she?" I marvel as we peer down at her.

"She is," he agrees.

We're so smitten. Dylan can't keep his eyes off his daughter, and really, neither can I. We're so in love with our little Autumn. She gives us sunshine and blue skies every day. And she's brought us even closer by giving our lives a shared meaning and purpose.

So when all is said and done, she really is our "embrace the unexpected."

I guess Graham was right all along. The little pamphlet he gave me a long time ago really has changed my life.

For the better…and for forever.

And you know what?

I wouldn't have it any other way.

## THE END

Are you ready for Jaxon's story, *Player on Ice*? It's coming this summer.

# ABOUT THE AUTHOR

S.R. Grey is an Amazon Top 100 and a #1 Barnes & Noble bestselling author. The bestselling Boys of Winter hockey romance series, the popular Judge Me Not books, the award-winning Promises series, the Inevitability duology, A Harbour Falls Mystery trilogy, and the steamy Laid Bare series of novellas are among her works. Ms. Grey's novels have appeared on multiple Amazon Bestseller lists, including the top 100 several times. She's also a #1 Bestselling Author on Barnes & Noble and a Top 100 Bestselling Author on iTunes.

**S.R. Grey Facebook:**
http://www.facebook.com/SRGrey

**Author Website:**
http://srgrey.com/

**Sign up for S.R. Grey's exclusive-content newsletter:**
http://mad.ly/signups/106801/join

**S.R. Grey on Twitter:**
https://twitter.com/AuthorSRGrey

**S.R. Grey Goodreads Author page:**
http://www.goodreads.com/author/show/6433082.S_R_Grey

**S.R. Grey on Instagram:**
http://instagram.com/authorsrgrey#

**S.R. Facebook Reading Group (join now for giveaways galore!):**
https://www.facebook.com/groups/SRGreyHardAbsandHotBooks/

# ACKNOWLEDGEMENTS

Thank you to all the readers, the bloggers, and everyone who loves and supports this series. You are amazing and I couldn't do this without you.

Thanks to Christopher John for the stunning cover photo, and to Najla Qamber for designing book covers that so perfectly capture the feel of the series.

Thank you, Franci N., for beta reading and always providing valuable feedback. I appreciate you and your insights. And Chloe thanks you for keeping her from wearing socks with her fancy dress.

Thank you also to Kristin S. and the editing team at Hot Tree Editing. And thank you to Julie Deaton for always stellar proofreading.

Heidi gets a shout-out for helping me brainstorm when I was stuck.

Lastly, thank you to my family and friends, and to my esteemed hockey "consultants."

Y'all make this journey possible.

It's not over yet.

Here's your chance to read the first chapter of **Destiny on Ice**, Brent Oliver's story and the first novel in the bestselling *Boys of Winter* series.

# GOLDEN BOY GETS A LITTLE TARNISHED

## BRENT

My father was a great hockey player. Back in the day, in the era of eighties' big hair and synthesized music, Billy Oliver won not just one, but two Stanley Cups. He was awarded the Conn Smythe trophy both times and has received an assortment of other hardware throughout the years.

He's retired now, but my dad was once a star.

To me, though, he's always just been Dad.

But as his only child, I have a legacy to live up to. I pray I don't disappoint him. I pray someday I'll be as good as he once was. And damn it, I better win a freaking Stanley Cup like he did.

I have no choice, not really. Since the moment my father first laced up hockey skates on my three-year-old little feet, the look of pride on his face told me even then all I needed to know—anything short of being the best will never do.

And guess what?

In many ways, I've become the best at what I do, which is, like my dad, play professional hockey.

I've been good since the start, a natural some say. I don't know about that, but I do know that even before I was drafted—in the first round by the Las Vegas Wolves, an expansion team at the time—I was being called "The Golden Boy" and "The Next One."

These days, three years later, I'm pretty much the poster boy for the NHL. And I have a slew of endorsement deals to prove it.

Lately, though, I've been falling short.

And I really don't know why.

Something is missing for me in the game. Or is it something that's missing in *me*?

I blow out a breath and shake my head.

Things started out so great. Where'd it all go wrong?

I made a name for myself early on. Expansion teams usually struggle for years before posting a winning record. Not so for the Wolves. With me centering what was then a subpar line, I was still able to make us shine. We came out swinging that first season in the league.

### BRENT OLIVER SCORES THE GAME-WINNING GOAL IN HIS AND THE WOLVES' FIRST NHL GAME, SETS UP TEAMMATES FOR TWO MORE

One month later, there was this:

### THE WOLVES OFF TO A COMPLETELY UNEXPECTED STELLAR START

Then things started to slide.

Those subpar players on my line weren't enough to keep afloat a pretty much overall crappy team, even with me centering. The Wolves' owners and management made the necessary moves—they don't mess around when shit needs to get done.

We picked up a phenomenal winger, Nolan Solvenson. He started to play and things turned around.

## ADDING SKILLED RIGHT-WINGER NOLAN SOLVENSON TO ROOKIE BRENT OLIVER'S FIRST LINE PROVING TO BE A MASTERFUL MOVE

### ON A MID-SEASON WINNING STREAK, THAT SOLVENSON TRADE IS PAYING OFF FOR THE WOLVES!

Another trade made at the deadline gave us Benjamin Perry. A big, strong left-handed winger, he was the final piece to the puzzle. Even with far-from-elite second, third, and fourth lines, it didn't matter. Not with me, Benjamin, and Nolan on the first line. We could *not* be stopped.

Benjamin—or Benny, as he's known to the team—is adept at using his size and muscle to check the hell out of any sorry soul who happens to be matched up against him. He simply wears other players down… and then it's a fucking scorefest. Thanks, in part, to his killer slapshot.

Together with Nolan, a sniper in his own right, we were—and in many ways still are—quite a force to be reckoned with. We destroy teams, though not as much lately. But back then, man, we were racking up so many points that the press branded us the OPS line, as in Special Forces.

### THE OPS LINE'S SNIPERS OF OLIVER, PERRY, AND SOLVENSON ELIMINATE THE COMPETITION WITH EASE

### THERE'S NOTHING COVERT ABOUT THIS LINE'S SCORING PROWESS

We worked our reputation to our advantage. Trash-talking on the ice and taunting players became our pastimes. We also happened to get a lot of pucks in the net.

*Ah, the good old days.*

We still trash-talk and taunt, but we aren't as lethal as we once were.

"We just need to get back on track," I murmur to myself. "The season doesn't start for a few more weeks. I'll have my shit together by then."

I better, since I'm the captain of the team. If I go down, we all sink. And that's not fair to anyone, especially not to my linemates, Nolan and Benny. Over the past couple of years they've become my best friends, which is a blessing and a curse. It's a blessing that we play so well together, but it's a curse that we also have a tendency to fuel each other's vices.

God knows this off-season we've become far too focused on partying and women. Like me, my linemates are extremely popular. Hell, let's not mince words—we're gods. In the hockey world, it's good to be a god. Guys want to *be* you and girls want to *do* you. Multiply that all by a hundred if you're not an ogre in the looks department.

And none of us are.

Not to brag—though, I guess I kind of am—but I have the most women falling at my feet. Hell, I've had women who've wanted to *lick* my feet.

Like, literally.

There was this crazy bitch this one time…

Wait, I digress. Back to where our team is today—floundering in a sea of mediocrity.

After that first good regular season, we fell apart during the playoffs. A dirty hit that sent me flying into the boards also sidelined me with a concussion. It didn't end there. More bad luck plagued our team. Nolan went into a scoring slump, and Benny took a punishing check against the boards that broke his foot. We were knocked out of the playoffs in the first round.

I went to Minneapolis, my hometown, to sulk.

"Next year will be different," my always-positive father tried to reassure me.

He was wrong.

We missed the playoffs entirely the following year, for reasons still unknown.

Then there was the season that just ended this past spring—another disappointment.

## LAS VEGAS WOLVES FOLD, KNOCKED OUT ONCE AGAIN IN THE FIRST ROUND

Needing a break from all things desert-life, I said to Nolan and Benny, "Fuck this shit."

That was over three months ago. We were in the middle of cleaning out our lockers for the summer. My linemates looked at me, confused.

And then Nolan finally asked, "Fuck what shit, Oliver? What are you going on about over there?"

"Everything," I replied, gesturing around the empty locker room. "We're done, finished. Let's get the hell out of this place for a while."

I meant Las Vegas the city—and I think Nolan was catching my drift—but Benny misunderstood.

"Dude," Benny began, "we *better* get outta here soon." He checked his watch. "We have a tee time at two."

He meant the golf game we had planned, but I was having none of that.

"Fuck golfing," I snapped. "I'm talking about *really* getting out of here. I think we deserve a much-needed break from this whole damn town."

Nolan looked intrigued. "What'd you have in mind?"

I happily shared with him and Benny what I'd been thinking about for days. "Let's head up to my house in Minnesota. We can spend the summer on the lake." I grinned, bad intentions in mind. "You know I'm a fucking rock star up there. We can party every night. Hell, we can fuck and get fucked up till training camp starts up in September."

Benny was in immediately, but Nolan had to think it over in his thoughtful kind of way.

At last, he said, "Okay, let's do it."

Since that day we've been partying like rock stars. Or, more accurately, like out-of-control hockey players.

We're still on a roll, even though it's August and we have to fly back to Vegas real soon. Until then, however, I've vowed my cool contemporary house by the lake will remain *the* place to party. It's our OPS base for debauchery, after all.

In reality, though, this craziness can't go on. We all know that.

Even wild and crazy Benny had the sense to ask me just last week, "Dude, what should we do?"

"About what?"

I was in the midst of texting a local puck bunny to see if she wanted to meet me for a quickie, so I was a bit distracted.

Benny sighed. "We gotta report to camp in a less than a month. Guess it's time to start thinking about slowing down with the girls, the booze, the—"

I put down my phone and cut him off with a raucous, "Hell no, my friend. We just need to scale it back a little."

"Scale it back in what way?" Nolan, who walked in the room just at that moment, wanted to know.

I shrugged. "Maybe have smaller parties? Maybe drink a little less?"

We all agreed to those things, but we haven't followed through. In the past seven days we've abstained from partying for all of two.

This is so not going to play well with the team. My diet is crap, and I'm nowhere near peak playing shape. Sure, my body looks all lean and cut, meaning you'd never know I wasn't ready to hit the ice rearing to go, but looks can be deceiving. I went out for a run just the other day and came back fucking winded as hell.

That was a first.

Still, I'm confident I can get back into playing shape in no time. It's the inside of my head that's kind of a mess. I just don't fucking care about winning, not anymore. I mean, I do, but I don't. Does that make sense?

Nah, it doesn't to me, either. But I better figure it out, and fast.

*Where's my drive to get my shit together? Where's my commitment to winning, my obligation to my players?*

I ask myself these things every day now, but I guess the answers are clouded by my drinking copious amounts of alcohol and fucking way too many puck bunnies.

*Dad would be so proud—not.*

Well, he would be glad I diligently use protection. I haven't gone *that* far off the rails. Still, wrapping my dick up isn't enough to keep management off my ass. My agent already informed me—this morning, in fact—that the Wolves' ownership group has a pretty good idea of what I've been up to, along with my teammates, here in Minneapolis.

I listened half-heartedly when my agent woke me up to say, "Don't blow this off, Brent. Management is *not* happy with you. There's a certain image they expect you to uphold, and you're not doing that."

God forbid I'm not the team's "Golden Boy." I'm "The Next One," remember?

*Bullshit, it's all crap.*

Coach Townsend called me shortly after I got off the phone with my agent. He had the same warning.

"You don't want the team to take action. You're not going to like what they have in store for you, Brent, if you keep up with this bad behavior."

"Oh, come on," I replied, laughing. "The Wolves can't fire me. And what could be worse than that?"

Coach T chuckled like he knew something.

*Hmm...*

"I can't worry about that shit today," I said to him. "I'll start cleaning up my act tomorrow."

"Brent..." Coach T sounded doubtful.

"Really, I will," I insisted.

That was a few hours ago. And I plan to make some changes. But maybe not quite yet.

"Before tomorrow gets here," I justify to myself, "we still have the rest of today. And that means there's time for one more party."

I stride into the second-floor living room of my house, a spacious and angled space overlooking the huge lake on my property. Peering out at the crystal blue water, I announce to Benny and Nolan, "Listen up, boys. We're having one final blowout tonight, a party to end all parties."

There's a murmur from Nolan, but nothing from Benny.

"We're going to do this one right," I go on. "We party tonight. But then, when tomorrow arrives, we're done with messing around. We start training full-on."

*Yeah, right,* a little voice in my head coughs out.

I look around since no one besides my guilty conscience seems to be chiming in.

It's early afternoon and the sun is bathing the room—my favorite, by the way, with the way it juts out over the lake showcasing the floor-to-ceiling windows on two sides and a massive deck with a mile-long view on the other—in a warm summer glow.

Nolan, who is lounging on an easy chair with a beer in his hand, raises his bottle. "I'm in," he says.

His words aren't the least bit slurred, even though he's been drinking straight through since last night's bash.

"And then, yeah," he continues, agreeing with me, "we'll start getting ready for camp."

Despite his ability to suck down alcohol like a fish, Nolan hasn't veered too far off course. Getting back on track won't be hard for him. He's like Mr. Discipline. And he's not fooling anyone, anyway. I caught him working out in my basement gym a few days ago. With the way he was pumping iron I suspect he's been training consistently for a few weeks now.

There's still not been a response from Benny, which is unusual. Dude's always up for a party. He's probably the worst of us when it comes to out-of-control antics.

And that's saying a lot.

"Hey, where's Benny?" I ask Nolan as I scan the shadows of the room.

He nods to a sofa that's been pushed way-ass off to a far corner.

"Oh, I should've known." I chuckle as I take in an eyeful.

Benny is sprawled out on a sofa in the shadows, sleeping like a baby. His massive chest is rising and falling in perfect rhythm with the ticking clock on the stone mantel above his head. Some puck bunny he was fucking around with last night is with him, passed out on top of him.

The sheet covering their naked bodies is hiked up just enough to afford a view of the girl's creamy thigh, which is casually slung over my linemate's muscular, hairy-as-hell leg, and positioned under his semi-exposed junk.

Chuckling at Benny's total lack of modesty, I pick up a throw pillow and lob it at his head—the one that clearly controls all his thinking.

*And he scores!*

As the pillow makes contact—and how could it not with a pole like that marking my target?—the sheet falls off completely. I get a quick flash of perky tits and tiny ass. And then, shit—a big honking piece of man-meat assaults my eyes.

"Dude," I snort, mock-offended. "You need to cover that shit before you blind us all."

Benny stirs to life. Sitting up, he barks, "What the fuck, Oliver? I was having the best dream ever. That is till you started tossing shit at my balls. "

Nolan lets out a low chuckle. "Only you, Benny, could find a way of using 'tossing' and 'balls' in the same sentence. But really"—he tilts his bottle to Benny's dick—"you need to do what Brent said and cover that shit up."

Throughout this entire brain-draining exchange, the girl wakes up. And damn, she looks young. Letting out a little squeak, not unlike a hamster, she gathers the sheet around her naked self and scurries off to where she seems to think the bathroom is.

I only know this 'cause she's muttering something about having to pee. But the poor girl has no idea where to go. Hamster-girl flies past me, heading down the wrong hallway, the one that leads to my bedroom.

As I rush to retrieve her, I can't help but grumble, "Why in the hell do they always think the damn bathroom's down *my* hall?"

I catch up to and redirect the girl, pointing her in the correct direction. "It's that way, sweetheart," I say in my kindest tone.

No need to be an asshole; the poor thing already looks shell-shocked. Though whether that's due to waking up in a strange house or waking up next to that monstrous thing Benny calls a cock, I have no clue.

"Thanks, Mr. Oliver," she replies.

And then she runs off.

"*Mr.* Oliver?" I shake my head. "What the fuck is up with that? If she thinks I'm old and I'm only twenty-two, then..."

*Whoa, wait.*

Hurrying back out to the living room and pointing an accusatory finger at Benny, I say, "That chick better be over eighteen, dude. We're in enough trouble already with the team."

Benjamin Perry is twenty-eight, but he likes younger girls. Nothing illegal, so don't get your panties in a bunch. He just happens to favor babes who either look young, or are *just* old enough.

"She's twenty-three," he replies, sounding hurt by my accusation.

"What? Five years past eighteen?" Nolan peers over at me and smirks. "Hey, Oliver, you think Benny is working up to go cougar on us?"

Laughing, I reply, "Seeing as he's on his way to fucking the full spectrum of girls in their twenties, I do indeed think he's secretly working his way up to thirty."

"Small steps," Nolan says.

"Fuck you," Benny interjects. "You're both dickheads."

I put up my hands. "Hey, don't be pissed at me. Take it up with Nolan. He started with the jokes. I only brought up the chick's age for your own protection. I'm always looking out for you, buddy."

"Yeah, you usually are," he concedes. "And thanks for that." He shoots me an apologetic grin. "You really are a good kid at heart."

I shrug, feeling a little self-conscious at being called a kid. But then I see what Benny is up to, preparing to bust my balls.

Sure enough, the next words out of his mouth are "You do know I mean *kid* in a good kind of way. Like maybe"—he smirks—"a *golden boy* sort of style."

"Ha. Ha," I retort. And since he's enjoying yanking my chain far too much, I shoot him the bird. "Shut the fuck up, man."

Benny may give me a hard time, but his underlying sentiment is genuine. What he said about me being a good guy, like a decent person, is true. Despite all the craziness of late, I want nothing but the best for my friends. And just because I've been fucking up my own life lately doesn't mean Benny's and Nolan's lives have to go down the shitter too.

Really, I probably should've never invited them to Minnesota. I should have come up to the lake house by myself. That would've been the smart thing to do, especially if my intention all along has been to piss away my career.

I don't really want that, though, do I?

No.

I just need some help in getting back on track.

But where would I find something like that?

*Ah, fuck it.*

"So what do you say, Benny?" I ask, back to focusing on the party. "You in?"

He stretches, covering his dick with the pillow I threw at him. I make a mental note to have all my furniture *and* their decorative accents, especially the pillows, steam cleaned.

Running his hand through his shaggy, dark blond hair, he says, "Am I in for what?"

"Party tonight," Nolan interjects in his usual no-nonsense tone. "One last blowout, and then Brent here says we're stopping with the bad behavior."

I have to laugh. Nolan is only three years older than me, but it's like he's twenty-five going on forty. He's the voice of reason in our crew.

Well, most of the time.

Not today, though. No, today he agrees to go all-out.

With the party plans full steam ahead, we get on our phones, texting and calling everyone we know.

"Tonight we party hard," I declare when we reconvene in the living room.

"Yeah," Nolan says, holding up a freshly opened bottle of beer.

"You mean hell, yeah," Benny corrects, raising the full shot glass in his hand.

"Hell, yeah," I echo, a beer *and* a shot on the table in front of me. "And just so we're clear," I add. "Tomorrow we give up the booze and the women. Tomorrow we start training for real."

The boys agree, and we drink to our plan.

*Yeah, tomorrow we'll do all those things…*

www.ingramcontent.com/pod-product-compliance
Lightning Source LLC
Chambersburg PA
CBHW020407210626
46816CB00006BB/2164